Love, Politics, and Red Velvet Cupcakes

Book Five of the Bex Carter Series

Tiffany Nicole Smith

Contact Me. I'd love to hear from you!
authortiffanynicole@gmail.com
Twitter @Tigerlilly79

Cover Designed by

Keri Knutson @ Alchemy Book Covers

Love, Politics, and Red Velvet Cupcakes

Book 5 of the Bex Carter Series

by

Tiffany Nicole Smith

My Journal

I've decided that when I grow up, I would like to be an award-winning photojournalist like my Aunt Alice. When I told her the news, she was thrilled because she loves what she does and she knew I would love it too. She gets to travel the world and see all kinds of exotic places, meet new people, and write about events that are important to the world. The best part is she promised that she would take me with her when she goes to Australia to cover a story this summer! I can't wait! But...there's a catch (there's always a catch ☹). In order to go I have to practice my skills by keeping a journal. I guess that's not so bad because I love to write, but Aunt Alice is going to read the journal so I have to be careful about what I put in it. Now don't get me wrong; Aunt Alice is the coolest adult I know. She's like a big sister to me, but she's still a grownup so she can't know *everything.* Some stuff is just downright embarrassing. Anyway, this journal will chronicle my eventful run for class president and an either tragic or wonderful love story. (Sorry, no spoilers!!!!)

1

The Great Doorknob Fight

#notmyfault

It was a quarter to ten when Aunt Jeanie dropped me off at school. School had started almost two hours ago, but I was late because of a dentist appointment. Eight o'clock that morning was the only time that Dr. Schroeder could fit me in and Aunt Jeanie didn't believe in going one day beyond the six-month deadline of getting a teeth cleaning.

"Do you want to be in dentures by the time you're thirty?" Aunt Jeanie asked.

According to her, I just *had* to go in that morning.

After going to the office to get a late pass, I headed to Mrs. Conway's social studies class. As I entered the 300 hallway, I spotted the last person I ever wanted to see—an evil creature named Ava Groves, aka Ava G., aka the meanest girl ever! Ava stood at the opposite end of the hallway and flipped her long black hair over her right shoulder. We stared each other down for a moment; then the two of us made a mad dash toward Mrs. Conway's classroom.

We both made it to the door and reached for the doorknob at the same time. I obviously grabbed the doorknob first because Ava G.'s hand ended up on top of mine.

She squeezed my hand. "Why are you late?"

"Not that it's any of your business, but I had a dentist appointment." I flashed a smile so that she could see my newly cleaned pearly whites. "Why are you late?"

"I had to see my dermatologist."

I tried to push her away from the door with my body. "The dermatologist? That's not an emergency."

Ava pushed me back. "It is when you have what looks like the beginning of a pimple. But what would you know? You obviously couldn't care less about your skin. Now let go!"

"No way! I was here first. You let go," I argued.

Ava's green eyes flashed with anger. "You let go, Bex Carter!"

I know, I know. It was such a stupid thing to fight over, but if you knew Ava Groves, you would understand. I was tired of Ava always getting her way. Every time she won, her ego inflated ten times larger than it already was, and the bigger her ego got, the worse her attitude was. Really, this was just my way of protecting the world from her evil powers. I'm kind of like a superhero.

Suddenly the door flew open, causing Ava and me to jump back. Mrs. Conway glared at both of us. "Ms. Carter. Ms. Groves. How nice of you to finally join us. And how nice of you to disrupt my class in the process."

"Sorry," we both mumbled at the same time.

Mrs. Conway opened the door completely and walked away, but we still hadn't learned our lesson. I couldn't let Ava enter the classroom before I did and she obviously had the same idea. The two of us squeezed into the doorway at the same time. Ava tried to push me back, but I was bigger and stronger than she was so I pushed her and made it through the doorway first. Victory!

"Ladies, please!" Mrs. Conway pleaded. The class stared at us in amusement and I suddenly felt stupid.

"Sorry, Mrs. Conway," I muttered again.

Ava G. rubbed her shoulder. "I think you dislocated my shoulder, Bex!"

"Girls! We are in the middle of a project. The assignment is on the projector. Grab a laptop and get started." Mrs. Conway headed for her desk and then stopped. "Oh, and by the way, this is a partner project and since you two just arrived, you'll be working together."

"Oh, that's just great!" Ava shouted sarcastically.

I silently agreed. Aunt Jeanie had picked the worse day possible to schedule a dentist appointment. I marched over to the laptop cart and grabbed one before taking an empty seat next to where Ava had settled in. I ignored the fact that she'd snatched the laptop out of my hands as I read the directions shown on the board by the overhead projector.

Think about some women from modern history who have roles similar to those of Nefertiti, Tiy, and Nefertari. Create a list of these women and their contributions; then make a graphic organizer that illustrates the similarities and differences between the contributions of the ancient Egyptian queens and the women from modern history. Choose one of those women to do a short presentation on.

We had been studying ancient Egypt all month. This week we had been focusing on Egyptian queens whom I found to be very interesting.

Ava G. grinned. "We should totally do Chanel Featherstone."

I didn't know much about Chanel Featherstone partly because I wasn't allowed to watch most things on TV, but mostly because I didn't care. She was famous for having a reality show, but from what I could tell, all she did was shop and talk about how beautiful she was. That girl was as shallow as a soda bottle cap. I could totally see why Ava would idolize her.

"No way. We're going to pick a woman who's actually done something important!" A great idea popped into my head. "I know. What about Val Ackerman?"

Ava gave me the stink face. "Nobody knows who that is!"

"That's the point. We can teach them something. She was the first president of the WNBA."

Ava stared at me blankly.

"You know, the Women's National Basketball Association."

Ava narrowed her eyes at me. "Don't you think about anything besides sports? We are *so* not doing that."

Okay, so I thought about sports a lot, but not all the time. Sports was something I was good at, so of course it interested me. "You can't just throw my suggestion away."

"Why not? You threw mine away."

I didn't realize that our voices were becoming louder and louder. Sometimes Ava makes me so angry that it's hard to control myself. "Because Chanel's an idiot. Val Ackerman is important."

Mrs. Conway looked up from her computer. "Ava Groves and Rebecca Carter…please. You only have fifteen minutes so I suggest you use that limited time a bit more wisely."

I cringed. She had called me Rebecca out of spite. Everyone who knows me knows that I hate being called Rebecca. I made a mental note to lower my voice, but I was not going to give in to Ava and spend my precious time doing a project on some superficial twit.

I placed the laptop in front of me. "You can do what you want, but I'm doing a presentation on Val Ackerman."

Ava G. pointed a pink pen with a ball of fluff on the end in my face. "Fine! I don't need that laptop. I know everything there is to know about Chanel right off the top of my beautiful pimple-free head." She would. "I'm doing my presentation on her."

"Fine!"

"Fine!"

We both worked quietly for the remainder of the fifteen minutes. By the time Mrs. Conway's timer had gone off, I had come up with quite a few interesting facts about Val Ackerman and the WNBA.

Mrs. Conway began going around the room and calling students up. Each pair had five minutes. I planned on speaking first and using up most of the five minutes, after all, my person was actually important to history.

"Ava Groves and Bex Carter," Mrs. Conway said, sounding really tired. I got the feeling that she wasn't expecting much from us.

Ava and I both left our seats and raced to the front of the room. I got there first (as I said before, I'm much faster than she is) and I began speaking as quickly as possible.

"Val Ackerman was the first president of the Women's National Basketball Association. She is currently—"

Before I was even done with what I had to say, Ava jumped in. "Chanel Featherstone is one of today's biggest media sensations."

I jumped back in, speaking faster and louder. "Val Ackerman is the current commissioner of the Big East Conference. She started off as a basketball player—"

"Chanel Featherstone just opened a chain of clothing stores in LA—"

"Val Ackerman was born in New Jersey in 1959—"

"Who cares? Chanel Featherstone was born—"

"Val Ackerman—"

"Chanel Featherstone—"

Mrs. Conway clapped her hands. "Girls, girls." Ava and I both stopped talking. The class stared at us as if we had turned green with purple polka dots. "The assignment was to focus on one person, not two. Part of the assignment was definitely not yelling over each other and cutting your partner off."

I had to let Mrs. Conway know whose fault this was. It was all Ava's. "I know, Mrs. Conway, but Ava wouldn't listen. Val Ackerman is a very important person in the women's sports world."

Mrs. Conway nodded. "I'm sure she is, Bex, but it's too bad we couldn't hear any of the facts about her because you were speaking so quickly. And Ms. Groves, you weren't any better. See me after class, girls."

Ava and I both dragged ourselves back to our seats. I watched the other groups as they worked together with their partners and delivered flawless presentations. Why couldn't I have someone I could get along with? Why did I always have to get stuck with Ava? It was bad enough that my aunt and her mother were best friends and the two of them always forced us to hang out.

The bell rang signaling the end of class and I reluctantly followed Ava G. up to Mrs. Conway's desk. I watched the other students file out of the room and wished I could be one of them. It was never a good thing when a teacher asked you to see her after class.

Ava flashed Mrs. Conway her famous, phony smile which I absolutely hated. Luckily, Mrs. Conway was one of the few teachers who saw through Ava's Little Miss Perfect act.

On top of the phony smile, Ava added a hair flip. "Mrs. Conway, I'm really sorry about Bex's behavior. I don't know what her problem is. She just gets so crazy sometimes."

The nerve.

Mrs. Conway sighed. "Ava, Bex isn't the only one at fault here. I'm going to have to hold you both responsible for that sad display of poor teamwork. And seeing as you weren't able to complete the assignment, I'm going to have to give you a failing grade."

Ava and I both sighed. Mrs. Groves expected her daughter to be perfect and bring home nothing less than an A, while Aunt Jeanie would send me to a boarding school in Antarctica if I brought home anything less than a B. So far, I was barely maintaining a B average in social studies and I needed that in order to go to Australia with Aunt Alice.

Ava began to hyperventilate. "Mrs. Conway, you cannot give me an F on this project. You just can't. I can't fail anything."

Really? She failed at being a decent human being every day of her life.

Mrs. Conway raised her eyebrow and I knew that she had something devious up her sleeves. "Well, there is something that you can do to save your grades."

"What?" Ava asked, leaning over Mrs. Conway's desk. "I'll do anything."

I rolled my eyes even though I was used to Ava's poor acting skills by then. Mrs. Conway looked at me. "Yeah, yeah, I'll do anything too—I guess."

Mrs. Conway pressed her hands together. "Great. Elections for the eighth-grade student council begin next week. If you run for one of the positions, I will raise your final grade a full letter. You don't have to win, but I do expect you to put maximum effort into campaigning and learning how school government runs. You can definitely use a lesson in citizenship."

I had no intentions of running for student council *ever*, but she did say that we only had to run, not win.

Ava thought for a moment. "I've always wanted to be president. I can see it now. Good morning, Madame President, the kids will say every day as I walk down the hallway. I already have the perfect dress to wear for my inauguration."

I couldn't believe this girl already thought that she had this election in the bag and it hadn't even started yet. I had no interest in being on the student council myself, but I knew enough about Ava to know that if she became the President of Lincoln Middle, I would beg Aunt Jeanie to send me to that boarding school in Antarctica.

2

Throwing My Hat in the Ring

—feeling undetermined ☹

Journal Entry #1

I don't have much to write today. I've just been asking myself when a certain person is going to stop ruining my life. No matter what I do, this certain person is always there trying to bring me down. I had no interest in ever being a part of student government, but now I have to because of this certain person! There seems to be no end to this certain person's evilness. Is this how Batman feels about the Joker?

That afternoon Chirpy and I lay on my bed reading the requirements for each student council position from the school's website. I closed my eyes as Chirpy read to me. "Okay, the responsibilities of the president are—"

"Pass. What's next?"

"Okay. The vice president—"

"Chirpy! Everyone knows VPs do more work than presidents. They're like the presidents' slaves."

Chirpy sighed. "All right, all right. Secretary. The responsibility of the class secretary is to attend all meetings and take thorough notes."

"No," I said.

"What do you mean, no? That sounds easy."

"Chirpy, my hand would cramp up and I would have to stay focused to take good notes. Do you have any idea how boring a student council meeting is? I'm not going to be able to pay attention."

"Bex, have you even been to a student council meeting?"

"No."

"Then how do you know they're boring?"

"I just knoooow. Trust me. What else is there?"

"Treasurer, but you're not that good with math."

"Chirpy, it's just counting money. I can add," I said.

"Okay. The class treasurer is responsible for collecting money for the eighth-grade account and keeping a running tally of gains and expenditures."

I get along fine with money. I could totally do that.

"The treasurer is also responsible for organizing fundraisers—"

"Next!"

"Bex, come on. None of these jobs is going to be easy."

"Chirpy, you and I both know that anything I try to organize is going to turn out to be a disaster."

She nodded in agreement. "Okay, the last job is class recorder. The class recorder's responsibilities are to read the minutes from the previous meeting and to make sure the meetings start and end on time."

I waited for her to finish reading the list. "Is that it? All I have to do is be able to read and tell time?"

Chirpy shrugged. "Yeah, that's all it says."

I sat up. "That's it! That's the perfect job for me. Bex Carter is running for eighth-grade class recorder, the easiest job there is."

Chirpy shook her head. "Shoot for the stars, Bex. Shoot for the stars."

The following Monday anyone who wanted to run for a position on the student council had to report to Mr. Hall's classroom after school. About twenty-five kids showed up. I wondered how many were running for class recorder. I just had to get that position. My social studies grade and a super-cool trip to Australia were at stake.

Just as the meeting was about to begin, someone took a seat at the desk behind me. The smell of mean almost overpowered my senses. I didn't have to turn around to know that it was Ava G. I rolled my eyes and prayed for the meeting to begin before she could say anything to me.

Mr. Hall stood at his podium with a pen. "Good afternoon, ladies and gentlemen. It's nice to see so many of you eager to participate in student government. I'm going to get an official list of who's running for what position. We'll start with the position of class recorder," he announced. "Who's interested in running?"

I raised my hand and another girl and a boy did too. Ava laughed behind me.

"At least you know what position losers are supposed to run for."

I turned to her. "It's not a loser position. It's a very important position."

"Yeah? Then how come only Scary Sherry and Frog Boy will be running against you? You know that's the only way you'll win, by running against bigger losers than you."

"I'm not a loser and you'd better stop calling me that. I'm a *winner*."

"No, Bex. I'm a winner. Watch me win this election. I'm going to be president and I'm going to make your life miserable. You and your little weirdo friends will want to transfer before the month is out."

"Yeah?"

"Yeah."

I narrowed my eyes at her. "Well, you can't win, because I'm going to be president and I'm going to make this school better and your life miserable."

Ava scoffed. "No one in his or her right mind would vote for a walking disaster like you. You would turn this school into World War Three."

I turned around quickly. Before I could even think about what I was saying I blurted out, "Mr. Hall, scratch that. I'm going to be running for president instead."

Somebody should really tape my mouth shut.

Chapter 3

The Campaign Trail

—feeling confused ☹

Journal Entry #2

So, it looks like I'll be running for class president. I'm not really sure how that happened, but it did. I think it's mostly because my mouth blurts things out before my brain can tell it to shut up. Also, I always feel the need to prove a certain person wrong instead of just ignoring her. I really need to work on that.

Aunt Jeanie hugged me like a boa constrictor squeezing a mouse, almost cutting off my circulation.

"I am so proud of you, Bex, for doing something so ambitious. I guess I'm finally rubbing off on you."

"Sftthhhhhhjjjjjjj." (Which meant, "Sure Aunt Jeanie." But my mouth was buried in her arm pit.)

Finally she let me go. She looked so proud of me that I didn't have the heart to tell her the truth. I'd only become involved in the election to save my grade and I was only running for president to challenge Ava. When I thought about it, the whole thing sounded pretty bad.

Aunt Jeanie began to fuss with my hair. "We have so much to do. We need to get you a campaign wardrobe. Maybe tame this hair—just a little. We have to write your speech, your campaign agenda—"

My eyes glazed over as Aunt Jeanie spoke. This was going to be a lot more work that I'd first anticipated. I thought I'd just hang up some posters, write a quick speech, and call it a day.

The doorbell rang and Sophia the housekeeper rushed past us to answer it.

"Hello, Sophia," said the visitor. I shuddered. That was the voice of Mrs. Groves and I was pretty sure that her horrible daughter was with her.

I was correct. Mrs. Groves marched in carrying a box and Ava waltzed in behind her.

"Jeanie, I just have to show you what we had made up for Ava's campaign," Mrs. Groves said as she placed the box on the dining room table.

Ava and I glared at each other. I had seen enough of her for one day.

"Oh, what's Ava running for?" Aunt Jeanie asked.

"President, of course," Mrs. Groves replied.

Aunt Jeanie folded her arms across her chest. "What a coincidence. So is Bex."

Mrs. Groves looked surprised then she turned to Ava. "You didn't tell me that Bex was also going to be running for president."

Ava shrugged. "I guess it slipped my mind. It's not like it matters."

Oh, Aunt Jeanie, when will you see how awful this girl is and stop forcing me to hang out with her?

Mrs. Groves looked at me as if I were some kind of wounded puppy. "Bex, do you really want to do this? I would hate for you to be disappointed."

"What does that mean?" Aunt Jeanie asked.

Yeah. What *did* that mean?

Mrs. Groves shook her head and smiled. "Nothing, just that my Ava is very popular."

Aunt Jeanie put her arm around my shoulder. "Well, everyone knows Bex."

Yes, everyone knew me, but that wasn't the same thing as being popular. It meant that I had been involved in several fiascos that everyone heard about. It didn't mean that they would vote for me.

"I'm just saying," Mrs. Groves continued, "Bex might be biting off a little more than she could chew. A class president has to be responsible, organized, personable—"

Aunt Jeanie tightened her grip around my shoulder. "Bex is all those things."

I so was not.

Mrs. Groves threw her hands up. "Listen, I don't want to fight. I'm just trying to help." She picked her box up from the table. "Anywho, since Bex is Ava's opponent, I guess we will have to keep our campaign ideas a secret."

"Fine," Aunt Jeanie said. "Good luck."

"Why don't you keep your luck? I have a feeling Bex is going to need it," Mrs. Groves said. No wonder Ava was so awful. Apple, meet your tree.

Aunt Jeanie squeezed my shoulder even tighter. I appreciated her sticking up for me but her grip was starting to hurt. "We'll see about that. You should never underestimate the underdog. Especially when the underdog is my niece. Good afternoon, ladies."

With that, both Ava and her mother smirked at us before leaving with their box of secret goodies.

Aunt Jeanie turned to me as the front door closed. "Bex, losing is not an option; you will win this election. Now grab some paper and a pen and let's start making our plans."

I was grateful for Aunt Jeanie's help, but I couldn't help but think that this was more about her proving Mrs. Groves wrong and less about me.

"We must get red velvet cupcakes from the Sugar Shack. They're the best in town."

I wrote that down. "That's going to be a lot of cupcakes, Aunt Jeanie. Hundreds."

"Not a problem," Aunt Jeanie said. "If we want to win against Ava, we're going to have to go all out. We will spare no expense."

Let me explain something about my family. My life is maybe a little…complicated. I live with my Aunt Jeanie and Uncle Bob. Aunt Jeanie is my mom's oldest sister.

Aunt Jeanie and Uncle Bob are also super-rich and my aunt has no problem letting the world know it.

My little sister Reagan is eight and a handful, but not as big a handful as Triple Terror, Aunt Jeanie's triplets: Francois, Priscilla, and Penelope. They're eleven, but thanks to Aunt Jeanie's babying them, they act like six-year-olds. Thankfully, I've lost the "privilege" of babysitting them because Aunt Jeanie doesn't think I'm responsible enough to look after her precious treasures, which is just fine with me.

Where are my parents? Long story short—my father is in jail for allegedly stealing money from his job, but he should be out soon. My mom took off before Dad even went to jail and is floating around Europe somewhere. I've kind of given up on her coming home. For now Aunt Jeanie and Uncle Bob are our legal guardians.

Anyway, Aunt Jeanie and I used to get along like oil and vinegar. I thought she hated everything about me, but lately things have been much better between us, although we still have our issues. I've learned to focus on the good parts of Aunt Jeanie and to be thankful for all she's done for me and Ray.

"So," Aunt Jeanie said, looking at her laptop. "Let's see…what do kids like? How about T-shirts? Dog tag chains? Bracelets?"

"That sounds cool, Aunt Jeanie." She wasn't joking about going all out.

"Okay. I'll put a rush order on these and then we'll start working on your campaign agenda."

"Uh, okay, Aunt Jeanie."

She continued to rattle off a list of things that *we* needed to do for *my* campaign.

"Bex, did I tell you that I was the president of my freshman class?"

"No, Aunt Jeanie."

"Well, I was and I won by a landslide so I know how to win a campaign. We need to—"

She kept talking as she left the room and went into Uncle Bob's study. I couldn't hear her anymore and I wasn't sure if she wanted me to follow her or not, but seconds later she reappeared with a book.

"We're going to beat Ava so bad Mrs. Groves is going to wish she never challenged us," Aunt Jeanie said as she practically threw the book at me. If I didn't have such good reflexes, it would have hit me square in the face.

"Uh, Aunt Jeanie, you know I'm not Mrs. Groves, right?"

She frowned for a moment; then her expression softened. "Oh, I'm sorry, Bex. I was just lost in thought."

I looked down at the book that had almost knocked my lights out—*The One, Two, Threes of Politics*. "Aunt Jeanie, you just happened to have this book just lying around?" I swear she had a book for everything.

"Of course. Bex, life is just one big game of politics. You'll find that the tips in those books can carry over to your everyday life."

I held the book up. It looked mighty thin. Now, I loved to read, but books that I wanted to read, not books that had been thrown at me by my aunt. I would definitely be skimming and picking out the important points.

Aunt Jeanie sent me to my room and demanded that I get started immediately. I spent the next couple hours highlighting the tips that stuck out to me. By the time I was done, I had come up with this list:

1. Be the voice of the people. Speak their language.
2. Come up with a catchy slogan.
3. Stand out.
4. Win people over in groups.

5. Be kind to everyone, especially the other candidates.

6. Be prepared to work hard improving your school.

I figured that I could do all those things until Aunt Jeanie burst into my room and made me all nervous again. "Bex, once we write your speech, I'd like to hear you practice it once or a few times. Tomorrow I'll go pick up a few power suits for you. I know Ava's campaign wardrobe is going to be impeccable and I won't have you looking like you're not even trying. And we *will* do something about that hair—"

And yada, yada, yada. I had the sinking feeling that this campaign was going to be a lot more than I had bargained for.

4

Campaign S.W.A.G.
(Stuff We All Get)

throws a T-shirt into a crowd of my adoring fans

Journal Entry #3

Campaigning is a whole lot of work. I know you've said that journalists have to leave names out of stories sometimes to avoid trouble, but I think you'll know who I'm talking about anyway since she's your sister. Aunt Jeanie is being very helpful, but it might be too helpful. I know she wants me to win, but she acts as if I'm

running for the President of the United States. If I lose, I think she'll be more disappointed than I will.

The official campaign period began a week later. When I told Aunt Jeanie I had planned on designing posters, she laughed in my face and had large banners made up at the local printers. Unfortunately, Mrs. Groves had the same idea for Ava so the hallways were completely covered in pink and purple banners that read "Vote for me, Ava G" or yellow and green signs that read "Be Smarter. Vote for Carter." (I came up with that all on my own.)

Step 2: Come up with a catchy slogan. Check.

Four kids were in the running for the office of president. Me, Ava G., Kristen Lee, and Harry Kline. Kristen Lee, the one person Ava G. probably hated more than me, was the leader of another clique of mean girls. As unbelievable as it may sound, Kristen could be even worse than Ava at times. I didn't know much about Harry Kline other than he was a nice, quiet boy and really smart. If this turned out to be a popularity contest, Kristen or Ava was destined to win.

The day after I told Aunt Jeanie I was running for president, she wanted to call a meeting with my campaign staff. When I told her I didn't have, she told me I'd better get busy putting one together because I wouldn't be able to do anything without a group behind me.

I have the best friends in the world because they came running at the drop of a dime when I needed them.

"We weel do anyzing for Bex to ween," Marishca said in her heavy Russian accent. Marishca Baranov was one fourth of The Tribe and the best gymnast I knew. Her body was like a rubber band. I was sure she would be in the Olympics someday. She was short and skinny with shoulder-length blond hair, which she tied back into a ponytail.

"But does Bex understand how much work this is going to be?" Lily-Rose asked. Lily-Rose Johnston was my sensible friend, although she could have a bad temper when someone pushed her too far. Her black hair was loose and flat-ironed which was something her parents had only recently begun to allow. Before she'd only been allowed to wear her hair in two braids She pushed her lavender glasses up on her nose. "I mean, being president of the entire class is a big job with lots of responsibility and sometimes she can be a lazy slug."

"Hey!" I shouted. "You do know that I'm sitting right here."

"It's not so much that she's lazy," Chirpy said. "It's just that she sometimes has problems focusing. I gave her the list of responsibilities to look over, so she knows all that she has to do. Right, Bex?"

"Uh, yeah, I'll look over that tonight."

Chirpy groaned. "Bex, you're going to be the death of me." Chirpy's real name is Beatrice. We called her Chirpy because she had a large nose that looked like a bird's beak. We gave her that name in kindergarten and it just kind of stuck. Chirpy always has a way of sounding like someone's grandmother.

I had three guy friends whom I would also ask to help—Santiago, Jeeves, and Maverick—but for the time being, I was just focusing on my besties.

Aunt Jeanie came into the living room with a typed list. I wondered if she had spent the whole day on this. "Okay, girls, I've given you each a job to do. I will be the campaign manager, meaning that I will make sure Bex's campaign runs effectively. Chirpy, you will be in charge of communication, which means that you will oversee the press and advertising related to the campaign."

Chirpy raised one eyebrow, but said nothing.

Aunt Jeanie continued. "Marishca, you will be the field department. That means you will research the school's needs and policies so that Bex can incorporate them into her platform. And last but not least, Lily-Rose, you have a very, very important job. You will be Bex's scheduler. That means you'll set up her appointments and help her keep up with important times. Also you will make sure she has things that she needs like water, ChapStick, et cetera, et cetera."

My friends stared at Aunt Jeanie as if she were speaking a foreign language; I wasn't sure that she wasn't. She was taking this whole thing way too seriously.

I cleared my throat. "Thanks, Aunt Jeanie, but don't you have to get the triplets to their cello lessons?"

She looked at her watch. "Yes, I sure do since Sophia's gone with Reagan to her dance class. I'll leave you girls to start discussing things and we'll touch base later."

"Okay, Mrs. Mahoney," my friends muttered as she left the living room.

"Okay, forget all that," I said.

"Chirpy, you're going to pass out the T-shirts. Lily-Rose, help me with the cupcakes. Marishca, you can pass out the dog tags. I'll ask Santiago to work on some graphics since he's good at that stuff and Maverick can be my hype man. I'll have Jeeves do my intro since he's always wearing a tux. I think I have the perfect campaign staff."

My friends looked relieved.

"Don't worry, Bex," Lily-Rose said. "We are going to rock this election."

The next day, the fun began. Tuesday morning my crew and I handed out my swag. Everywhere I looked, kids were wearing "Be Smarter, Vote for Carter" T-shirts and dog tags with my face on them. A line for red velvet cupcakes stretched down the hallway. Ava G. had brought chocolate cupcakes from some fancy French bakery, but everyone knows that those are no match for a red velvet cupcake from the Sugar Shack. I made each kid promise to vote for me before I handed him or her a cupcake.

Albert Finley licked the strawberry frosting on his cupcake. "Hmm. American Buttercream. Your dessert palate is very sophisticated. Can I have two if I can get the entire cooking club to vote for you? There are twenty-two members and I'm the president. They'll do whatever I tell them to."

This was exactly what I needed to do—make connections with the other leaders in the school. I reached into the box and handed him another cupcake. "Deal. I'll be counting on your votes." I made a note in my binder that I had the cooking club's vote. Aunt Jeanie would be very proud of me.

Ava G. trotted down the hallway followed by her posse of Avas: Ava T. and Ava M. They were all wearing matching T-shirt dresses with Ava's campaign slogan printed on them. I had to admit that it was cute although I would never tell them that.

Ava stopped in front of me. "Bex, nice try. Too bad your auntie's money can't buy you popularity."

"Whatever, Ava. Like my Aunt Jeanie said, never underestimate the underdog."

"Yeah, well never overestimate the overdog," Ava M. said. Clearly Ava G. was the brains of the group.

"That makes absolutely no sense," I told her.

Ava G. poked her in the arm. "Yeah, shut up. When I need you to talk, I'll say so."

Ava M. looked hurt. She had only been trying to stick up for her friend, but I couldn't feel too sorry for her. She chose to hang out with Ava and she was always mean to me and my friends.

"Let's go. I don't want the smell of loser to cling to us. It doesn't mix well with my Chanel Featherstone body spray." Ava sneered at me before walking off with the other Avas.

The more she insulted me, the more I was determined to win this election.

5

Promises, Promises

—feeling optimistic ☺

Wednesday was "Meet the Candidates" Speech Day. A debate between the candidates would be on the following Monday and voting would take place on the next Friday. I needed to tell my classmates what I stood for and what I would do for the school. Mr. Hall had met with all the candidates and told us that we needed to choose a platform. What would we focus on to make the school better? Academics? Social Programs? I decided to focus on sports and athletics.

Aunt Jeanie had kept her promise and found me what she thought to be the perfect candidate wardrobe. That day she insisted that I wear a navy blue dress suit she had found because according to her, navy was the new black and a classic color. I reminded her that I was trying to win over a bunch of thirteen-year-olds, not senior citizens, so she had me wear a zebra print top underneath to jazz it up. I still thought that I was dressed like someone's mother. The outfit was definitely not Bex-like and I felt uncomfortable in it the entire day.

Once all the eighth-graders had gathered in the auditorium, Principal Radcliff pulled a name from a hat to see who would go first.

"First up is Ms. Kristen Lee," he announced.

Each candidate would have two minutes to speak. We were to simply introduce ourselves and state why we felt we would make a good class president.

Kristen stepped onto the stage wearing a plaid dress suit, but hers looked a lot cooler than mine. She had her long dark hair parted in the middle and pulled back into a ponytail. I had to admit that she looked very presidential.

"Dear fellow eighth-graders, it is an honor to stand before you today. If you choose me for your class president, I promise you that I will make this the best year ever. There will be a dance every other week. I will make Fridays movie Fridays, and since Mondays are so rough on us, I will have lunch catered from The Burger Palace every Monday, just for eighth-graders of course."

She paused and everyone applauded. I looked down at my note cards wondering if what I had written, with Aunt

Jeanie's help of course, would get that same kind of reaction.

"Thank you," she said before taking her seat.

"Thank you, Ms. Lee," said Principal Radcliff. "Next up we have Ms. Ava Groves."

I groaned louder than I meant to from my seat on the side of the stage. I could only imagine what she was going to say.

Ava was dressed in a very expensive-look jumpsuit and heels. With that outfit and her long hair done in spiral curls, Ava looked great, but not like a president. She definitely didn't look like a kid in middle school. "Dear fellow rock stars…"

She'd just started, but somebody please, make it stop.

"This is our very last year of middle school before we go into high school and we need to make this the best year ever. If you elect me to be your quee—president, I promise to make this a year you will never forget. First, I will make everything in all the vending machines free. Whatever you want, all you have to do is press a button. I will set up game stations in the morning and during lunch with all the hottest video games. Fridays will be Fashion Fridays. I will turn our hallways into runways where we can showcase the latest fashions—like this jumpsuit from the Victor Vitoli

Spring Collection. My father is personal friends with him and I always get a peek at new things before they go public. In the bathrooms, I will add vanity mirrors with good lighting and makeup and perfume for us to freshen up during the day. If you've been lucky enough to have been invited, you know that I throw the best parties. Every dance we have under my presidency will put any other dance to shame. Last but not least, I will have Chanel Featherstone come talk to our school on Career Day."

I rolled my eyes. Sure, the girl who has no career. Unfortunately, Ava killed it. As she exited the stage, almost everyone gave her a standing ovation. She got even bigger applause than Kristen had. Maybe she was a rock star.

I looked at Harry Kline who sat beside me nervously fiddling with the buttons of his suit. He looked back at me and shrugged, shaking his head. I think we both knew that neither of us stood a chance. My idea of having a mini-sports Olympics was going to seem like nothing compared to what Ava and Kristen were promising. Aunt Jeanie was going to help me come up with ideas for health and nutrition to go along with my platform. After what the kids had heard so far, my speech would put them to sleep.

"Next up, Mr. Harry Kline."

Of course I would have to go last. I felt sorry for Harry. Ava's speech was going to be tough to follow.

Harry walked slowly to the podium, his hands shaking as his held his index cards. He took a deep breath and began his speech.

"Dear fellow students, I know many of you don't know me, but my name is Harry Kline. Student government has always been a passion of mine. I was the president of my fifth-grade class and I'm also the vice president of my Wilderness Boys troop. I have plenty of leadership experience."

The auditorium was dead silent. There was no clapping or cheering, but everyone was listening to him. Even without the crazy promises, something about Harry got their attention.

"I love this school and I have a lot of ideas on how to make it better. For one, I'd like to start a peer tutoring club where students tutor other kids who need help. This will serve two purposes—students will get the help that they need and the tutors will get credit for the service hours we need to pass the eighth grade. Also, I'd like to raise funds for new athletic equipment, both for PE and for our teams to use. If you elect me, I'd like to come up with other social activities for us besides dances. I mean, dances are fine and we will still have them, but there are some kids like me who are just not into them. There should be other activities for us to enjoy. I have plenty of other ideas, but my time is up. I hope you elect me and give me a chance to serve as your president."

I placed my cards on my lap and applauded Harry. He had been honest and genuine. Everyone in the audience clapped for him, although he hadn't received the hoots and yells Kristen and Ava had gotten.

I braced myself waiting for Principal Radcliff to call my name.

He shook Harry's hand and walked over to the podium. "Next up, Ms.—"

"Next up, is Beeeeeeex Carter!" Jeeves yelled. He had run up on the stage and grabbed a spare microphone sitting on the stand. His voice was so loud that it echoed off the walls of the auditorium. Half of the kids broke into giggles.

I had forgotten that I'd asked him to introduce me. Jeeves took a bow, straightened the jacket of his tux and then walked off the stage. I know it may sound like it, but Jeeves isn't some kind of whack-job. He wears a tuxedo every day because he wants to be an orchestra conductor when he grows up so he dresses the part. His name is actually Walter, but everyone has called him Jeeves since elementary school because he looks like a butler.

Principal Radcliff cleared his throat. "Thank you, Walter, for that boisterous introduction. Ms. Carter, the floor is yours."

I stood on wobbly knees after Principal Radcliff announced me. Some kids were still laughing at Jeeves' introduction and I wished they'd stop so I wouldn't feel as if they were laughing at me. As I walked to the podium my friends screeched my name like crazy, making me feel less nervous. At least I knew I had them in my corner.

I stood at the podium and took a deep breath. I had an important decision to make. Would I read what I had written on my cards or would I try to outdo Ava and Kristen?

I quickly decided that to beat them, I had to join them. I had to make these kids some promises that they would get excited about.

Ava and Kristen had promised some really cool things, so I had to make my promises extra cool. "Hey guys. You know me and I know what would make this school better and a lot more fun for all of us. First, I would start by setting up an all-you-can-eat ice cream sundae bar in the cafeteria, just for eighth-graders. Then on days when it's really hot, I'll have those giant inflatable water slides brought in for PE—and laser tag every day."

I looked around the auditorium. Everyone was smiling and nodding. Now I had to make my promises bigger and better. I couldn't forget to mention how I was going to improve student learning. "I'm going to add a new sport to our curriculum—horseback riding. We can hold a fundraiser for horses and a stable. For field day we can add go-cart racing and the biggest, best promise of all, instead of going to Washington, D.C. for our annual eighth-grade trip—we will go to Australia!"

Everyone stood and the auditorium erupted with applause. They couldn't even wait for me to finish my speech. I knew right then and there that I had won that round. I looked back at Ava and Kristen and they were seething. They knew that I had blown their speeches out of the water. I took a bow, feeling very proud of myself and took my seat off to the side of the stage.

Principal Radcliff went to the podium. "That concludes our first round of very…interesting introduction speeches. I would like to see Ava, Kristen, and Bex in my office immediately after this."

I could only imagine what he was going to say. Maybe he was going to give me the position of president right on the spot. It was obvious by the students' reactions that I was the people's choice.

"Have a seat, ladies," Principal Radcliff said as the three of us entered his office.

"Is there a problem?" Ava asked.

He took his glasses off and rubbed his eyes like he always did when he was tired. "Yes, there's a problem—a big one with all your speeches."

"What's wrong?" I asked.

"For starters, those promises you made, they're all impossible. There's no way our school could afford to do any of those things aside from the fact that they're ridiculous. You can't turn the school into an amusement park."

"We could hold fundraisers," Kristen suggested.

"Those fundraisers would have to raise hundreds of thousands of dollars and that just doesn't happen. Really? A trip to Australia? Fashion shows in the hallways? Catered lunches?"

"Principal Radcliff, my mother has always taught me to dream big," Ava said smugly.

"I'm all for dreaming big, but those things are just not going to happen, nor do they have anything to do with improving the school."

"What are you saying?" I asked.

"I'm saying no more crazy promises. At the debate I want you to discuss real issues that actually pertain to the school. Take a look at Harry. What he said was right on target."

Kristen rolled her eyes. "But his speech was so boring."

"No, it was honest and realistic. I mean it. Focus on the issues and give the students something reliable that they can depend on. Would you want to be lied to and made a bunch a promises that couldn't be kept?"

No, I wouldn't. He was right. If I wanted to win I had to focus on the real issues—beating Ava and Kristen.

6

The Power of Politics
—feeling confident ☺

Journal Entry #4

In the book Aunt Jeanie gave me, it said that sometimes politicians running for office have to make promises they know they will never keep. It's part of the game. That doesn't sound right to me. But...it was in the book so I did it anyway.

I took a look at my checklist and figured that I was doing a pretty good job getting things done.

3. Stand out. Check

I figured that I had already done that no matter what else happened. Also my swag and red velvet cupcakes had been a big hit.

1. Be the voice of the people. Speak their language. In progress

This step would require the most work, but I was already on the job.

So far, I had the cooking club and all the kids who had promised me their vote when they took a cupcake. I know that some of those kids could have simply been lying to receive a cupcake, but I had faith that most of them would keep their promise.

Friday morning I hunted down Adella who was the captain of the soccer team. I was on the soccer team, so I was pretty sure that I had their votes, but I had to be sure. Ava and Kristen could be very crafty and may have done something to try to win them over.

"Good morning, Adella," I said as I handed her a warm bagel. Aunt Jeanie had picked me up a box on the way to school. She said that food was a good way to win people over. "Here's a little something to help you get your day started right."

Adella took the bagel gratefully. "Thanks so much, Bex. I didn't have time to eat breakfast this morning." She unwrapped the bagel and took a bite.

"Adella, as a fellow Lady Cougar," (that's what we called the girls who played on sports teams) "I hope that I can count on your vote as well as those of the other girls on the team."

"Of course," Adella said. "Do you know that Ava G. had the nerve to try to get our votes? She promised us new uniforms—ones with glitter and sequins. Who needs that? All that shiny stuff would be totally distracting."

"So what did you tell her?" I asked.

"I told her no way. That our loyalty lies with Bex."

"Good. Thanks so much," I said, before turning to walk away.

"But," Adella said, grabbing my shoulder. "If you are elected, what are you going to do for the soccer team?"

I sighed. "New equipment. We've been needing new balls and goals for a while. I'll make sure we get those."

Adella grinned. "Promise?"

"Of course," I answered. "If I say I'm going to do it, I'm going to do it."

"Thanks, Bex. Good luck," she said as she walked away.

I was going to have to write all these promises down. I took out my binder.

Promised Votes:

1. The cooking club: Albert wanted an extra cupcake. (Done—I wish they were all that easy.)

2. The girls' soccer team: new equipment

After I was done with Adella, I went to find Brice who was the captain of the boys' soccer team.

"Of course you have our vote. We're family. This is a brother and sisterhood!"

Uh, no, Brice. We just play the same sport, but whatever. I went along with it. "That's right. We are family. A great big soccer-playing family and I promise to get the teams all the new things they need."

"Cool," Brice said. "And we could really use some new soccer cleats, the kind the pros wear."

Yikes! Those could be hundreds of dollars a pair, but I took my binder out and wrote it down. "I'll see what I can do."

"Awesome, Bex! I hope you win. Ava and Kristen don't care about soccer. And Harry, I think we all know he doesn't stand a chance of winning."

He was right. If Ava or Kristen won, the only sport that would get any attention would be cheerleading. "All right, Brice. See you later."

I was on my way to find Brittany, the president of the glee club, but I needed to make a quick stop to grab my notebook for first period. I opened my locker and grabbed my blue notebook. When I shut the locker door, I almost jumped out of my skin.

Scary Sherry and Frog Boy were just standing there staring at me. If you ever saw Sherry, you would know right away why she is called Scary Sherry. She is ghostly pale and skinny with black, black thin hair that always covers her face. It doesn't help that she is super-quiet and always manages to pop up unexpectedly and scare the living daylights out of people.

"Hey, guys. What's going on?" I asked, putting on my friendliest smile.

"We want to help you out," Frog Boy said.

I hate to admit it, but I had forgotten what Frog Boy's name was a long time ago, mostly because everyone called him Frog Boy and he answered to it. I didn't have any classes with him, so I never heard teachers call him by his real name.

Frog Boy got his name because his tongue is abnormally long and he allegedly uses it to catch flies. Now, I've never seen how long his tongue is—nor do I want to, but I have seen him eat a fly before. He did it in the cafeteria. A fly had been circling his lasagna. He just grabbed it with his hand and ate it like it was nothing. Gross, right? Trust me, it took all the willpower I had to not barf up my own lunch.

"You guys want to help me?" I asked. I was surprised because I had never said more than ten words to either one of them.

"Yes," Sherry answered. "Ava and Kristen are big fat liars. They promised both me and Frog that if we voted for them they would make sure we won the position of class recorder."

Class recorder. I remembered when I was going to run for that position. It would have been so easy and stress free. Nobody really cares who the class recorder is. I think most kids do eenie-meenie-minie-moe when they vote for that position.

"Obviously," Frog Boy said, "they're lying to one of us."

"Or to both of us," Sherry added. "They don't care about this position. I doubt they'd do anything to help either of us win." Then Sherry looked at me. "That's why you have my vote. You're real and honest. I trust what you say."

I swallowed hard. "You do?" I thought they were giving me way too much credit.

Frog Boy nodded. "Sure, your campaign speech was a little over the top, but you have a lot of charisma. We want to be a part of your campaign team. Those girls cannot win."

I put my arm around Frog Boy's and Sherry's shoulders. "That's great to hear. Welcome to Team Carter."

Sure, they were weird, but they were also really nice and if I wanted to beat the two most popular girls at school in this election, I needed all the help I could get.

Ava was a cheerleader so I figured I wouldn't even bother asking for their vote. Since I was the underdog, I decided to band the other underdogs together. There were way more of us than there were popular kids.

The downside to that was that time was running out, so I had to delegate some of the networking to my campaign team. Lily-Rose and Jeeves were working on getting all the band votes. Santiago said that he had the computer club leaning in my direction, but Ava had promised them lots of new high-tech gear. Marishca would work on the gymnastics team and Chirpy the nature club.

Maverick told me that the aquatics club was in my corner. Who even knew that we had an aquatics club?

"Yeah, mon. We meet on the weekends sometimes and go snorkeling," Maverick said.

So, I ended up having to promise the aquatics club a field trip to the beach on a school day. The band wanted new mics. The nature club wanted more binoculars for their scenic hikes. The gymnastics team wanted new mats and the computer club wanted something that I'd never even heard of and couldn't pronounce.

Whew! Principal Radcliff was right. Keeping these promises was going to be expensive. We would have to do a lot of fundraising. Thankfully, that was the job of the treasurer, not the president.

I finally managed to find Paisley Thomas, who was president of the art club. She was in the art room cleaning paint brushes. The art club had plenty of members so getting their votes would help a lot.

"Hey, Paisley, what's going on?"

She laid a handful of brushes on a paper towel. "Hey, Bex. How's it going?"

"Good. Pretty busy. I've been wanting to talk to you about the election."

"Oh, yeah—" Paisley began before we were interrupted by something that sounded like a screeching cat. I turned to see Ava dragging Albert Finley into the room by his ear. I told you the girl was a monster.

"Tell her!" Ava ordered.

Albert winced in pain. "Sorry, Bex. I can't vote for you."

"Why not?" I asked. "We had a deal."

Ava finally let go of his ear.

"I know, but Ava offered me something better than an extra cupcake. She promised to have Montgomery Winston, the world-renowned chef come and teach a cooking class for us. What could I say to that?"

"You could have said, 'No thank you, I already promised my vote to Bex and I have to keep my word.' How about that?"

Albert bowed his head looking truly sorry and I felt bad for him. Ava could be downright frightening. "I'm sorry," he said.

I glared at Ava. "She couldn't care less about the cooking club. Do you really think she's going to bring that chef here?"

Albert shook his head. "No—ow, ow, ow, ow, ow!" Ava had grabbed his ear again and he quickly changed his tune. "I mean, yes! If Ava makes a promise, she's going to keep it."

I pushed her hand away from Albert. "Stop it!" Then I turned to Albert. "Get out of here before you lose an ear."

Albert nodded and ran from the room as if he were being chased by the big bad wolf.

Ava turned to Paisley and gave her the biggest, fakest smile I had ever seen on a person. "Paisley, just the person I wanted to see."

It was crazy how she could go from torturing someone one minute to being sickly sweet the next. But Ava had been unusually nice the whole week, except for what she had just done to poor Albert, and I knew it was all part of her campaign plan.

Ava looked around the art room. "I've always loved art. I even thought about joining the art club for a long time."

"Then why didn't you?" I asked.

"Shut up, Bex! I'm talking to Paisley," she shouted.

If I had a penny for how many times Ava told me to shut up, I would have been a kazillionaire a long time ago.

Paisley wasn't stupid. She put her hand on her hip. "Really? Because you've always said that the art club was for dorks. The only time you even speak to me is when you're calling me a dork. You even wrote that in your blog."

Ava's smile dropped just a little. "Oh, that? That was the old Ava Groves. The new Ava has turned over a new leaf. No more mean girl. This mean girl has gone nice."

Paisley narrowed her eyes at Ava. "Is that so? Because what you did to Albert about ten seconds ago wasn't very nice. I know what you're doing, Ava, and it's not going to work. The art club has already decided to vote for Bex. She looks out for the little guy."

Go, Paisley!

Ava G. could never handle being told no because she was the world's biggest brat. She scowled at Paisley. "See, I tried to be nice, but apparently being nice gets you nowhere. If you don't get your club to vote for me, this will be the first club I shut down. I'll just say there's no money in the budget and use the money in the art club fund to go toward new cheerleading outfits."

Paisley looked a little bit afraid, but I didn't want her to back down. "She can't do that, Paisley. Only Principal Radcliff has the power to shut a club down and he would never do that."

Ava stepped closer to Paisley and stared deeply into her eyes. Paisley stared back wide-eyed as if she were in some kind of trance. Ava might be some kind of evil sorceress. "Don't underestimate me. My mother is the president of the

PTA and she can make anything happen. If I say the word, this stupid, boring club will be history."

"Okay, okay," Paisley said. "I'm sorry, Bex. Real sorry."

I narrowed my eyes at Ava. In less than five minutes she had stolen two clubs from me. Maybe she was better at this politics thing. Threatening people seemed to work a lot better than winning them over. Why wasn't that in the *One, Two, Threes of Politics*?

Step #7: If someone refuses to vote for you, impose threats or bodily harm.

There were lots of things I wanted to say to Ava, but I still had other groups I needed to reach out to and arguing with her was going to get me nowhere.

Unfortunately, by the time I had talked to the glee club, the chess club, the debate team, the junior honor society, and the track team, Ava had already gotten to them. Everyone seemed afraid of her and wouldn't even think of not giving her their votes. If Ava G. won this election, she wouldn't be a president. She would be a super-evil-controlling dictator. She might have been securing a lot of the votes, but I wasn't about to give up and let her win.

After school, Natalie Jackson, the president of the glee club pulled me to the side. She was whispering and making me kind of nervous.

"Please don't tell Ava," she said. "If I didn't promise her our votes, she said she would make us sing nothing but nursery rhymes for the rest of the year and I believe she can do it. She always gets her way."

I rolled my eyes. Nursery rhymes? That girl was unbelievable. "I'm sorry about that, Natalie, but I understand."

I turned to walk away, but Natalie grabbed my arm. "No, I told her I was going to vote for her just to get her off my back, but I'm not. I'm voting for you."

"You are?"

"Yes. I believe that you can make things equal and fair for all of us. The presidents in the past have only cared about cheerleaders, the basketball team, and dances, but someone like you will look out for all of us. Look how terrible Ava's acting and she hasn't even won yet. Bex, for the good of the school, you have to win."

I was flattered and slightly ashamed. "I'll do my best, Natalie." Right then something changed. I wasn't just trying to beat Ava anymore. I really wanted to win this election because I felt that I could really change things. People were depending on me.

I was more determined than ever to become eighth-grade president.

When I got home I tried to brief my campaign manager (Aunt Jeanie) on how things were going so far. I found Aunt Jeanie outside yelling at the pool boy in Spanish. He just shook his head and seemed to be ignoring her. Who knew what Aunt Jeanie was saying to him?

"Hold on just a second, Bex," Aunt Jeanie was saying when a bloodcurdling scream came from inside.

Some people might have been alarmed by that sound, but when you lived with Triple Terror and Reagan Leigh Carter, you heard noises like that all the time. I've learned to tune them out.

Moments later, we heard another scream that was even louder than the first one. Aunt Jeanie sighed. "Bex, Sophia's out running errands for me. Will you see what's going on up there?"

I groaned. That was like asking me to walk into a lion's den. They were always up to something ridiculous. I found it was best to leave them alone and they would eventually solve their own problems or beat each other up.

"Please and thank you," Aunt Jeanie said, pushing me toward the door.

I dragged myself up the stairs slowly, dreading every step. Sounds of a struggle came from the girls' room. I opened the door to find Priscilla, Penelope, and Reagan wrestling each other on the ground while Francois pounded a gavel on the desk yelling, "Order! Order!"

I put my pinkies in my mouth and whistled. Everyone froze.

"What is going on here?"

Reagan pulled herself from underneath Penelope. "We were having an election and nobody voted for me."

That was when I saw it. Taped around the room were pieces of construction paper that said either "Hey, hey, vote for Ray" or "Princess Priscilla for President."

"Penelope, what's going on?" I asked.

She rubbed her elbow. "Priscilla and Reagan were running for President. Francois and I voted for Priscilla and Ray went all crazy."

Ray frowned and folded her arms across her chest. "It's not fair. They only voted for her because she's their sister."

"That's not why," Francois said. "Ray said that if she became president of the house, she would be the queen and make us all her slaves."

I could see that. Even though she was younger, Ray managed to boss the triplets around.

"Yeah," Penelope added. "She said that she would make us do her chores and massage her feet and eat all her vegetables for her. Why would we vote for her?"

I looked at my sister. "Is that true, Ray?"

"Well, yeah, that's the whole point of being a president. To boss people around," she answered.

I had to set her straight right then. There was no way I was going to let my little sister grow up acting like Ava or Kristen. "No, Ray, that's not what a president does at all. When you become president, the people don't work for you; you work for the people. You have to make sure that things are fair and that everyone is getting what they need."

Ray scowled. "That sounds super boring, Bex. Why do you want to be president so bad then?"

I thought for a moment. I couldn't tell her the truth about why I'd initially run—to prove Ava wrong. "Because, Ray, I think I can do a good job and make the school better. It might be a lot of work, but I'm sure it'll feel great knowing that I'm making a difference."

Ray looked like she understood a little bit. "I guess I don't blame them for not voting for me. I wouldn't vote for me either."

Priscilla stood on her bed. "Now that we have that settled, my first order of business as president of the house is to enforce the Pink Law. That means everyone in this house must wear something pink every day, even you

Francois. Right now, except for Penelope, each and every one of you is in violation!"

I sighed as I prepared to give my cousin the same talk I had given Ray.

7

The Blackout

(It totally wasn't my fault. It really wasn't this time.)

Journal Entry #5

I wonder if I will ever stop being a disaster-magnet. No matter what, catastrophes seem to find me, and my poor friends always have to pay the price. Sure, I could have just walked away, but then a certain person would have gotten away with her rotten behavior once again. She had to be stopped!

The next day campaigning was going pretty smoothly. Quite a few kids had actually told me they were going to vote for me. A lot thought I was a normal kid like them, as opposed to Kristen and Ava who acted as if they were the queens of Lincoln Middle.

Lily-Rose and her boyfriend and my friend, Maverick, better known together as MavRose, had come up with quite a catchy song for me. The two of them were musically gifted so I wasn't surprised when they had created such a beautiful melody. I was touched that they had gone through all that trouble for me, especially when I hadn't even asked them to.

I had gotten permission to play my campaign song over the PA system once during lunch break. I thought it was very nice of Principal Radcliff to allow me to do that.

Ava G. on the other hand was having none of it. I think she had little spies set up all over the school because somehow she had heard about MavRose writing a song for me.

In the main hallway she had a system set up where she blared this horrible song that I could tell had taken her all of thirty seconds to make up. Ava might have been a beautiful dancer, but a singer she was not. I mean seriously, could no one in her camp have told her that she sounded like a dying ostrich? It was so bad that I almost felt sorry for her.

"What am I supposed to do now? She's totally drowning out my song." I asked Jeeves and Santiago as we stood in front of my locker shielding our ears.

Jeeves, who was actually wearing a Vote for Carter shirt under his tux, put his hands on my shoulder. "Bex, if there's one thing I know about politics, I know that you have to fight fire with fire. If she's drowning out your music, you need to play it louder."

"Okay, but how?" I asked.

Santiago backed away. "I have to get to the computer lab. I have an idea."

I didn't have time to ask him what his plan was because he took off down the hallway telling me to trust him.

A minute later Ava's music suddenly stopped and the lights when off in one section of the main hallway.

"Hey, what gives?" Ava shrieked.

A girl named Amber came running in my direction.

She stopped, breathing hard, trying to catch her breath.

"Amber, what's wrong?"

"You have to get to the cafeteria now. You've got to see what's playing on the TVs in there."

So many bad thoughts went through my head as I followed Amber to the cafeteria. What was playing? I could only imagine what Ava had done now.

When I reached the cafeteria I quickly discovered that it wasn't Ava at all. My song was blaring from the TV along with my slogan "Be Smarter, Vote for Carter" scrolling across the bottom. Santiago had somehow gotten hold of the system that's used to broadcast the morning news and set that up. I wasn't surprised. He had been running his own website design business for a couple years. The kid was a technological genius.

As you can imagine, Ava was not about to take this lying down. She came into the cafeteria with her mic and decided to do a live performance. I was pretty sure that everyone wanted to stuff the bread pudding in their ears to make the torture stop. It was so loud that I couldn't hear myself think. How was I supposed to come up with a plan of what to do next if I couldn't think?

Just then, everything turned dark. There was no light, no sound, no anything. The electricity had gone out.

For a few moments no one said anything and then Randy Andrews shouted, "It's the end of the world!"

Now Randy had issues—I've always known that about him—but no one else had a reasonable excuse for what happened next.

Danny Brisco yelled, "Black out! That means no school!"

Then everyone screamed and went crazy as if school had let out for the summer. I couldn't believe that darkness could make everyone lose their minds.

In all the chaos I was shoved into the hallway where I pressed myself against the wall for safety.

"Uh, oh," Santiago said from behind me.

"What happened?" I asked.

"I had one of the kids from the computer club get to the circuit breaker to cut power off to the hallway where Ava was playing her music. She figured it out and sent one of her people to turn the power back on, but obviously someone got confused and cut the whole school's power off."

Before I could say anything, Principal Radcliff's voice roared over a bullhorn. "Everyone, freeze!"

Emergency lights came on in the hallways and kids began to calm down. There was light, but not nearly as much as when the electricity was on. Just then, the bell rang, telling us that lunch was over. "Everyone back to class! Ava Groves and Rebecca Carter, to my office."

"Oooooooohhhhh," swept over the hallways as kids made their way to their fifth-period classes.

By the time I was seated in front of Principal Radcliff's desk, the electricity had come back on.

"What do you two have to say for yourselves?" he asked.

"I didn't do anything," I said. I really hadn't. "You gave me permission to have my song played over the PA system. Then Ava tried to torture everyone with that terrible excuse for a song that she had just made up. She was drowning out my song."

Ava sat up straight in her seat trying to look like the innocent person that she wasn't. "Principal Radcliff, you said that we would all have equal time to campaign. Bex was allowed to play her song, so I should have been allowed to play mine."

"Then you should have played it after school," I told her.

"When everyone's leaving and not paying attention? That wouldn't have been fair." She looked at Principal Radcliff with these wide puppy-dog eyes. "Isn't this supposed to be a fair race?" He nodded and I rolled my eyes. This girl was a pro at playing the victim. "Anyway,

Bex was drowning out *my* song so I had to turn up the volume. I was only trying to have my voice heard, Principal Radcliff."

He sighed and rubbed his eyes, probably wondering how many days he had left until he retired. "This isn't about the songs. It's about the power getting shut off. That was extremely dangerous. In all that chaos, someone could have gotten hurt. How did that happen?"

Ava and I both shrugged. I really didn't know what to say. I knew someone had turned the power off to a section of the main hallway to help me out, but I wasn't about to throw him and Santiago under the bus.

"I honestly don't know," I told Principal Radcliff.

Ava stayed silent.

Principal Radcliff folded his arms across his chest. "Fine. I'll just check the surveillance camera and see who went into the electrical room. Then I'll call the police."

Ava sat forward. "The police? Just because the power went out?"

Principal Radcliff nodded. "As I said, this person caused a very dangerous situation."

I couldn't tell if Principal Radcliff was bluffing or not because he was very good at it, but I didn't want to take any chances with the police.

"Fine, fine," Ava blurted out. "I asked someone to turn the power back on to the hallway but only because Bex had someone turn the power off in the first place."

Principal Radcliff looked at me.

"Look, I didn't tell anyone to do anything. It was their idea."

"Whose?" Principal Radcliff asked.

I didn't want Santiago or his friend to go to jail. I looked down at my hands. "I can't say."

"I won't either," Ava said, which was unusual for her. This was a girl who would have snitched on her own mother to keep herself out of trouble.

Principal Radcliff sighed. "Girls, I really hate to do this, but you've left me no choice. I have to pull you both out of the running for class president."

Ava clutched the front of her blouse and leaned back in her chair as if she were going to pass out. "No! You can't do this to me! I worked so hard! I was going to win! I know it!"

Although I wasn't nearly as dramatic as Ava, I was crushed. The thought of being the class president had grown on me, not only because I wanted to beat Ava, but because I thought I could actually bring some good changes to the school. Now that would never happen.

Principal Radcliff shook his head. "I'm sorry, girls, while I appreciate your enthusiasm, blowing out the school's power was just too much. Since you won't tell me who's responsible, I'm going to hold you responsible. The class president is supposed to set a good example for the other students. Neither of you have been doing that."

I wanted to cry, but I would take my consequence like a woman. I knew the worst part would be telling my friends—no, the worst part would be telling Aunt Jeanie, but telling my friends would be bad too. They wanted this and had worked just as hard as I had. I hated letting them down, once again.

Just as I expected, everyone was waiting for me outside my sixth-period class. Chirpy, Lily-Rose, Marishca, Santiago, Jeeves, Maverick, Frog Boy, and Scary Sherry. I couldn't even look them in the face.

"So what happened?" Lily-Rose asked.

"Ava and I got disqualified. I'm sorry, guys."

Everyone groaned.

"Man," Santiago said. "The poll on my website showed that you were in the lead with 38 percent of the vote. Ava G. was right behind you with 35 percent. You were probably going to win, Bex."

I knew Santiago was trying to make me feel better, but he was only making me feel worse. "I guess Kristen's going to win now. I'm really sorry, guys. Thanks anyway for supporting me."

Santiago patted my back. "Don't worry, Bex. You'll still be Madame President to us."

Everyone else nodded in agreement. I wasn't going to be president, but I had the best friends in the world.

8

The Sting of the Queen Bee

—feeling doomed ☹

Journal Entry #6

The worst thing that could possibly happen happened. I'm not going to win the election, but not because I didn't get enough votes—because I got kicked out of the running. The whole thing is totally unfair. I didn't ask anyone to mess with the school's power, but I still got blamed for it. I guess Nana has been right all these years. Life just isn't fair.

Other than breaking the bad news to my friends, the worst part had been telling Aunt Jeanie. She had invested a lot of time and money into this election and it had all been for nothing. After spending an hour on the phone trying to convince Principal Radcliff to change his mind, she finally accepted the fact that I wasn't going to be president.

Aunt Jeanie sat next to Uncle Bob on the couch where he was reading from his tablet.

"I'm really sorry, Aunt Jeanie. I know how you wanted me to become president like you were when you were in high school."

Uncle Bob burst out laughing, which surprised me, because I didn't think he ever listened to us when we talked. Maybe he had read something funny.

"What's so funny, Uncle Bob?" I asked.

He kept laughing. "You didn't tell her how you won?" he asked Aunt Jeanie.

She folded her arms across her chest. "It wasn't important. I won. That's the point."

"How did she win?" I asked.

"The other candidates got the chicken pox and had to drop out. She was the only name on the ballot and she only got seventy percent of the vote. The other kids wrote in the janitor's name," Uncle Bob explained. He was really getting a kick out of this, but Aunt Jeanie was not amused.

She shot Uncle Bob her famous look of death and he stopped laughing right away.

"Anyway, Bex, I'm sorry that happened but at least Ava can't win either."

Really, Aunt Jeanie? I couldn't have been too surprised by her comment. I had known all along that a big part of her wanting me to win had been because she wanted to prove Mrs. Groves wrong. But then again, who was I to talk? For most of the campaign period, I had been focused on beating Ava instead of running for the right reasons.

The cherry on top of the disaster sundae was that Principal Radcliff watched the video from the school camera and suspended the two boys who had messed with the power. Santiago had asked Kenny Shubert to cut the power off to the hallway. I felt guilty because he had only been trying to help me.

The next day at school, I came to a frightful realization. Now that Ava and I were out of the running, Kristen Lee was a shoo-in to become our class president and boy did she know it.

In light of what had happened, Principal Radcliff extended the election another week, to give students more time to make a decision. Instead of that Friday, the official voting would take place the following Friday. That gave Kristen one more week to gloat about how she had defeated us, even if it had only been by default.

"Ha, ha," she said as she glided by me one morning. "I knew I wouldn't have to lift a finger. All I had to do was sit back and relax and this election would fall right into my hands."

Ava and I got a rude awakening on Friday afternoon as we entered the locker room to prepare for gym class.

Kristen was standing on a bench giving an impromptu acceptance speech. "Listen, I heard about Santiago's poll and I know that you losers were going to vote for Bex and Ava G. over me. You'd better know that I'm going to make the rest of your middle school life absolutely miserable when I'm in power. Now, if you've been Team Kristen all along, your life will be gravy. I'll make sure that you have the best of everything while the peasants won't enjoy a single dance or fun activity as long as they are in this school. Mark my words."

One of her friends helped her step down from the bench while the rest of us shuddered.

"We really messed up," I whispered to Ava. "We've thrown the school under the mercy of that monster." Not that Ava would have been any better, but I didn't see the point of mentioning that right then.

Ava narrowed her eyes as she watched Kristen pass out stickers with her name on them. "Or maybe not. Kristen is not in office just yet. There's still someone running against her."

"Harry Kline? Are you serious? That poor kid doesn't stand a chance," I told her. "He's pretty much been invisible throughout this whole campaign."

"Bex, you give up too easily. We still have a week. A week to turn Harry Kline into someone the kids will vote for. Aren't you the one who always says to never underestimate the underdog?"

"Yeah, but you think we can do that in a week? We'd have to turn Harry into a completely different person and he'd have to go for it. I'm sorry, Ava, but that sounds impossible."

She turned and looked me dead in the eye. Don't tell anyone, but it scares me just a little when she does that. "Who do you think you're talking to? I'm Ava Fiona Victoria Groves. I can do anything. Are you in or not?"

I was still pretty unsure, but it was worth a try. "I'm in," I answered.

And just like that, Operation President Harry was underway.

Saturday afternoon Ava had invited Harry over to her house for lunch. When he asked why, she hung up on him without giving him an explanation. I was worried that he wouldn't show, but a couple of hours later, Ava, Harry, and I sat on the Groves' patio by the pool eating from the tray of sandwiches, or should I say Harry was eating while Ava watched him like a hawk. Every time I reached for a sandwich Ava would kick me under the table.

"Bex, these sandwiches are for Harry. I know that Reuben sandwiches are his favorite."

"How did you know that?" Harry asked once he had swallowed a bite. He didn't even talk with his mouth full, which was a lot more than I could say for other boys.

"I—I did my research," Ava answered, which was just a little bit creepy.

"Anyway," Ava continued. "Bex and I were thinking about the election. We're totally bummed that we can't run anymore, but if we can't win, we want the best candidate to win, and that is you without a question."

Harry beamed. "Thanks, that means a lot to me. But…I'm a realistic guy. I know I don't have a chance to win against Kristen. I never had a chance against any of you."

"Then why'd you run?" I asked. "Why go through all that if you know you're going to lose?"

"I wanted to get some of the important issues on the table. There are lots of changes I'd like to see before we graduate, not just for us, but for all the kids that come afterward. At least I'd give people something to think about."

"What kinds of issues?" Ava asked. "Dances? Cuter cheerleader uniforms?"

Harry snorted. "No, I mean real issues, not the foolishness you guys were talking about." Then he looked down at the table. "Sorry."

My cheeks burned as I thought about my ridiculous campaign speech. Harry was right. It was foolishness. He was the only one who really cared about the real issues from the beginning.

"Anyway," Ava said, flipping her hair. "We asked you here, Harry, because you are going to win this election and you're going to do it with our help."

Harry looked back and forth between Ava and me. "I appreciate you wanting to help me, but unless you possess some magical powers, I can't win."

Ava rubbed her hands together like some kind of evil scientist. "Harry Kline, I can take you and make you the most talked about and desirable boy at Lincoln Middle by Tuesday. By Wednesday, every girl is going to want to date you, by Thursday every boy is going to want to be you, and by Friday, you're going to win this election by a landslide."

Maybe Ava should go into politics. She was really convincing. I was starting to believe that she might actually pull this off.

Harry, on the other hand, looked pretty terrified.

"Harry, are you okay?" I asked.

He shook his head. "That sounds like a bit much. I don't want to be popular and the topic of everyone's conversation. This isn't really about me."

"But it is, Harry," Ava said. "If you don't win, you leave Lincoln Middle at the mercy of Kristen Lee."

I was reminded of her horrible speech in the locker room the day before. "Kristen is going to be the worst president ever. She's already promised to make us all miserable. If you really care about our school, you're going to do anything within your power to make sure that this girl doesn't win."

Harry sighed and thought for a moment. "She is going to make an awful president." He bit his lip. "All right. What have I got to lose? Let's go for it."

Ava stood and clapped her hands. "First, let's hit the mall and get you some new clothes and a new haircut. I'm also going to buy you that new cologne by Valducci. It drives girls crazy."

Harry looked even more afraid than he had before. "B-Bex, are you coming?" His voice almost sounded as if he were pleading with me to go along and save him from Ava.

Participating in one of Ava's makeover projects was about the last thing I wanted to do. I'd rather pluck off my own toenails and eat them. "Nah, you're in good hands. Besides, I have soccer practice in a bit."

Ava led Harry toward the house. "We don't need Bex for this. Fashion's obviously not her thing. You're in good hands with me."

Harry looked at me helplessly, but what could I do? He was in the right hands. If we were going to make Harry popular in less than a week, we needed to change his image. Loafers and sweater vests weren't going to buy him any votes. Neither was that soup-bowl haircut.

"Don't worry, Harry," I called after him. "You're going to look great."

Boy, was I right. On Sunday we had gathered in my bedroom. By we, I mean the Team Harry Committee we had formed. Harry's eyes bugged out when he saw the number of people who were on his side. Before, he had been only a one-man team.

My bedroom was pretty big, but with all the people crammed in, it seemed rather small. The Team Harry Committee consisted of:

Me
Ava G.
Ava T.
Ava M.
Chirpy
Lily-Rose
Marishca
Santiago
Maverick
Jeeves
Scary Sherry
Frog Boy

The boys were equally peeved with Kristen's antics. "Do you know that she said only the boys that she and her friends considered hot would be able to come to school dances and extracurricular activities?" Jeeves asked.

"Well, I guess that'll leave you out of everything," Ava T. said, chuckling.

"Hey, if you're going to insult people, you can leave." I couldn't stand the Avas, but for the time being we needed them. Regardless, they weren't going to be mean girls in my bedroom.

She looked at Ava G., who said nothing and then shut her mouth.

Anyway, back to Harry and his new look. I hate to give Ava credit, but she had done an amazing job with Harry. That day he was wearing skinny jeans and an oversized T-shirt. His hair was a little shaggy and fell just above his eyes. If you were into that kind of thing, you would actually think he was cute.

"So what's the next step?" Santiago asked as he typed something on his laptop.

Ava G. stood up and placed her hands on her hips. She loved having the floor. "We have four school days before the election and four things we need to do to make Harry the guy that everyone's talking about. Step one, we need to start a scandal surrounding him, something mysterious that will make everyone want to know more about Harry. Step two, we need to make him a hero. We're going to set up a situation where Harry will save someone. Everyone loves a hero. That will win him major points."

We waited expectantly for her to go on with the rest.

"Well, what are the other two steps?" Maverick asked impatiently.

Ava shook her head. "I think that's all you can handle for now."

What were we? Stupid?

"I'll share the next two after steps one and two are completed."

Everyone groaned but Ava waved her hands. "Trust me. I know what I'm doing. Now, to come up with a juicy scandal…"

9

Ava's Bright Idea

—feeling set up ☹

Journal Entry #7

It sounded like a good idea at the time. Little did I know that what started as a tiny snowball would turn into the giant avalanche that is my social life. Once again, I have a certain person to thank for this.

Miranda Phillips, the school's biggest gossip, grabbed my arm between third and fourth periods, practically digging her nails into my skin.

"Have you heard about Harry Kline?"

I pried my poor arm away from her. "No," I lied, "what about him?"

"His real name is Enrique Rodriguez and his family is in the witness protection program. Apparently, they witnessed some kind of gruesome murder and they're living here to hide out from the bad guys. Isn't that terrifying?"

"Yes," I said, pretending to be surprised. "Wow, who knew that quiet Harry Kline had such a big secret? Kind of makes me want to get to know more about him."

Miranda nodded. "You're right. I used to think that Harry was one of the most uninteresting people I knew, but that's all changed. He *has* to be quiet and blend in so that he and his family won't be discovered. He's been doing a really good job of flying under the radar."

It was too easy. Apparently, Ava actually knew what she was doing.

Step 2: Make Harry a hero.

Step two was also completed on Monday. Marishca, the one of us who was the least afraid of heights (and the smallest), was hanging a "Vote for Harry" poster in the gym when the ladder "slipped" from underneath her.

"Somebody help! Somebody help!" Chirpy yelled, as she ran through the hallways.

Everyone ran into the gym and gasped when they saw Marishca hanging from a bar right below the scoreboard. If I didn't know any better, I would have been frightened for my friend, but I knew that she could land on her feet without a problem.

Harry, who was looking especially cute that day, pushed his way through the crowd. "I got it. I got it."

He stood underneath Marishca with his arms out. They had practiced this, mostly for Harry. Marishca was a flyer on the cheerleading team and expert gymnast, so this would be nothing to her. Harry, on the other hand, had been scared that he wouldn't have been able to catch her. We had even put a piece of masking tape on the exact spot where he was supposed to stand.

He looked terrified at that moment. His voice shook as he spoke. "Okay, Marishca. I've got you. Just drop."

"No, I cannot," she said, sounding afraid. Who knew she was such a good actress?

"It's okay. I'll catch you. I promise."

The crowd of kids stood in silence, holding their breaths. Finally, Marishca let go and for a millisecond, I was worried that he might actually not catch her. That would be a catastrophe. What were we thinking?

But before I could finish my thought, Marishca had landed safely in Harry's arms and everyone was applauding. Harry placed Marishca safely on her feet and she gave him a peck on the cheek. Everyone patted him on the back and cheered until the janitor ran in yelling about how students were not supposed to be using ladders.

The crowd dispersed after that and I discovered the Avas leaning against the wall. Ava G. particularly looked very proud of herself. "Everything is going according to plan," Ava G. said as I approached. "We need to meet today after school. We have to kick things up a notch. Like my father always says—strike while the iron's hot."

And boy did we.

Monday afternoon the team met again in my bedroom. We were watching Ava pace back and forth. "Santiago, what do you got?" she asked.

He looked at his laptop. "My new poll shows that Kristen has 72 percent of the vote while Harry has 28 percent."

Ava pulled her hair. "Arggghhh. Is that all?"

Harry looked pleased. "That's pretty good. Before I only had two percent of the vote."

"It's better but not good enough. The good news is that it's only Monday so we still have three days to make this happen."

"So what's the plan? What's step three?" I asked.

Ava took a deep breath. Something about the look on her face told me that I wasn't going to like step three. "We need to make girls like Harry and the fastest way to do that is to give him a girlfriend. Make him part of a couple. Everyone will be wondering what she sees in him and he'll show them."

Harry turned bright red. "I-I don't really know about—"

Ava clapped her hands at him. "Harry, if you want to win, you've got to do what you've got to do. It's not a big deal. It's just pretend. Next week after you're president, you guys can have a big break-up."

"So…" Lily-Rose said. "Who's going to be his fake girlfriend, Ava? You?"

Ava stared at Lily-Rose for a few seconds. Then she laughed and laughed and laughed.

(Five minutes later)

"Woo-hoo," Ava said with her hand on her belly. "Lily-Rose, that was a good one, but seriously, we have to make it believable. If we try to get everyone to believe that

Harry's dating a girl like me, they'll know it's a sham. We need to give them something they'll buy. Any takers?"

The girls looked at each other.

Lily-Rose grabbed Maverick's arm. "Obviously, I can't do it."

"I'm going out wiz Caleb," Marishca said quickly.

"I'm going out with Mikey," Chirpy blurted out. She so was not, but before I could bust her, Ava M. cut in.

"How about you, Bex?"

"Me? What about you?"

She looked flabbergasted. "Did you not hear what Ava just said? This has to be believable."

"Look, it's all right," Harry said. The poor guy looked mortified. Who wouldn't? We were talking about him like he was a stinky piece of cheese that nobody wanted.

"No, I'll do it. I'll be Harry's fake girlfriend." I would have said almost anything at that point to put Harry out of his misery.

Ava G. sat down on my shag carpet with a satisfied grin. "Great! It's official. Harry and Bex are the newest couple at Lincoln Middle."

What are you waiting for? Please, tape my mouth shut!

10

The First Lady

—feeling confused ☹

Journal Entry #8

Why can't boys just say what they mean, and mean what they say?

S.S.S. (That means "sorry so short.")

"I'm glad that's settled," Ava said, pulling out her phone. "I'm going to send out a few texts. By tomorrow, everyone will be talking about the new couple and then on Wednesday you two will go on your first public date. We can't waste any time." Ava stood and pulled Harry over to me. "Stand up, Bex. I need to get a picture of you two." She pushed us together and snapped the picture before I was even ready. She looked at it and frowned. "I guess that's as good as it's going to get. Well, I have to get ready for dance class," Ava announced as she left and the other Avas followed behind her. After a few minutes, only Chirpy, Marishca, Lily-Rose, and Santiago were left.

"Santiago, are you going to update the poll for Harry's supporters?" I asked.

He slammed his laptop shut. "Tell your boyfriend to do it himself. I'm off of this stupid team. I have a business to run."

Without another word, he stormed out of my bedroom, leaving us all confused.

"What was up with that?" I asked. Santiago wasn't usually one to be moody; just a minute before he had been fine.

Lily-Rose sighed. "Bex, you couldn't get a clue if it bit you on the butt."

"What?" I asked. Chirpy and Marishca looked just as confused as I felt.

Lily-Rose looked at each of us. "Never mind."

"No," Chirpy said. "Tell us what you're talking about."

"Okay, but you can't repeat this. Maverick told me this in confidence and he wasn't supposed to tell me because Santiago told him this in confidence."

I was sitting on the edge of my bed. "Well, what is it?"

"Santiago likes you."

Everyone stared at me waiting for my reaction. I couldn't say I was too surprised. A while ago Santiago had told me that he thought I was cool and different from other girls so I kind of figured that he liked me then. But ever since, he'd acted like the same old Santiago and he treated me like the same old Bex, so I didn't know what to think.

Chirpy nodded as if she understood everything. "Of course. That's what he's upset about. You pretending to be Harry's fake girlfriend. He's jealous."

"Jealous of what?" I asked. "If he wanted to ask me out he could have. But he hasn't."

Marishca sat beside me on my bed. "Eez not zat easy, Bex. Eez hard to muster up zee courage to ask someone out. He's probably afraid of you rejecting him."

"Yeah, or making your friendship awkward," Chirpy added. "But—if he were to ask you out, what would you say?"

All eyes were on me again. I shrugged. I really didn't know what I would say. I had thought about it once and decided that I would have given Santiago a chance if he asked, but he hadn't so I kind of pushed the thought away. There was nothing that I didn't like about Santiago so I would probably say yes. I didn't tell my friends that though. "I don't know."

Lily-Rose stood and stretched her tiny body. "I think you guys make a great couple. He and Maverick are best friends and we could totally double date, but for the time being none of that matters. Until the election is over, you're Harry's girl and Santiago's not going to be happy about it."

Oh yeah. I guess at the moment I was Harry's girlfriend and starting tomorrow at school, I would have to act like it. I was really scared about that, but not as scared as I was about hurting Santiago.

Ava decided to give me a quick girlfriend lesson Tuesday morning in the girls' bathroom. She was speaking to me as if I were an alien from a distant planet, but deep down inside I was thankful for the advice. I wasn't sure if I could pull this off.

She ran her brush roughly through my mane of red, bushy hair. "Hold his hand. Laugh at everything he says as if it's the funniest joke you've ever heard in your life. Look deep into his eyes. Don't kiss him yet. We'll save that for tomorrow."

Eep! Kissing?

"Let everyone get over the shock that you're actually going out. Write his name on your notebooks and talk about him all the time."

I groaned. "How much work does it take to be someone's girlfriend?"

"Bex! I'm not even done! At lunch, feed him—"

"Stop! Stop! Stop! That's where I have to draw the line. I will never be feeding any boy. *Ever*."

Ava sighed. "Fine. At least dab the side of his face with your napkin. Even if there's nothing there, pretend that there is."

Nope. I wouldn't be doing that either, but I wasn't about to argue with her.

Ava looked me up and down and then handed me her brush. "Keep it. You need it more than me."

I slid the brush into the front pocket of my backpack as Ava pushed me toward the bathroom door. "I told Harry to meet you by your locker before school. Let's go."

I took a deep breath and allowed Ava to lead me to my locker as my head spun. Suddenly I was totally nervous and weirded out by this whole situation.

"There he is," Ava whispered as if I were blind.

Harry leaned against my locker sporting his new look and holding a red rose. I gulped and walked over to him.

"Morning, Harry."

"Morning, Bex. This is for you."

I took the rose from him as kids walked by staring at us. "Thanks."

"Can I walk you to class?"

"Sure."

He held his arm out awkwardly.

"What?" I asked.

"I want to carry your books."

"Um, that's okay."

A loud "arrgh" came from behind me—Ava clearing her throat. I had forgotten that she was there.

"Give him your backpack," she said between clenched teeth.

"All right." I handed him my backpack and he slung it over his shoulder.

I paused for a moment and then began walking to my first-period class. Everyone was staring at us and whispering but I guessed the point was to get people talking. Something incredibly uncomfortable happened as we rounded the corner. He grabbed my hand—and held it. My instincts told me to snatch it away, but then I remembered that I was pretending to be his girlfriend and handholding was something that couples did.

I was also thinking about Santiago. What would he think about this? He was my friend and I didn't want to upset him.

We stopped in front of my math class.

"Uh, well thanks," I said.

He nodded. "No problem. I'll meet you after class."

"Okay."

He stood there watching me as I walked into class. Inside, I sank into my seat and waited for Santiago to come in. He sat right next to me in social studies so I was kind of dreading it. The bell rang and class began, but there was no Santiago. I figured that he was late, but he never showed up, which was unusual for him.

After class I found Maverick and asked him if he knew where Santiago was.

"Yeah, he said that he wasn't feeling too good today so he was staying home."

"Oh," I replied. But I had a horrible sinking feeling that he had stayed home because of me.

11

First Dates and Paparazzi
#nopicturesplease

Ava arranged my and Harry's first date at the Pizza Shack. Harry wanted to have his mother pick me up, but I declined. I didn't need Aunt Jeanie asking questions about who was picking me up and why, so I told her that I was meeting the Tribe there and Sophia dropped me off. Why tell her about a boy I would only be dating for a few days?

Harry was already at a table waiting for me with a box of candy, which was really sweet of him. He wore a button-down shirt and slacks and smelled like my Uncle Bob.

He stood as I took my seat. "You look nice."

I didn't feel like I did, but I accepted the compliment. I was wearing a frilly green blouse with jeans and sneakers. Mostly, I didn't want to look like I was trying too hard; after all, this was only pretend, wasn't it?

I knew Ava would kill me once she saw what I'd worn, but I pushed that thought away.

The Pizza Shack was packed and I tried to ignore the fact that people were staring and taking pictures of us, but it was hard.

"Boy, Ava sure knows how to get the word around, doesn't she?"

I nodded. "Yeah, she's something else."

The waitress came over and Harry and I decided to share a small ultimate pizza and a pitcher of Sprite. After that, things got really awkward and silent.

I drummed my fingers on the table. Then I stopped, remembering that wasn't very ladylike behavior. "So, what's it like running for president?"

"It's actually kind of, especially now that I might even have a chance to win."

"You didn't think you had a chance before?"

Harry shook his head. "No way, not with you, Ava, and Kristen in the running. Before Ava helped me out and gave me this makeover and boosted my popularity, I didn't stand a chance. Even so, I thought it would be good practice for me. I want to go into politics when I grow up, maybe as a mayor or even a governor."

Wow. Harry really was the best person for this job. We had to make sure that he won.

Harry took a long sip of his Sprite. "Thanks for doing this. You didn't have to."

"No problem. It's not so bad. You're cool."

"Even though this isn't real, you're the first girlfriend I've ever had."

"Really?" I asked, but I wasn't really surprised. "I've had a kind-of boyfriend before but I guess you're my first real official boyfriend. I could do worse."

Harry smiled. "I hope I don't ruin your reputation."

"Harry, I don't know how much you know about me, but my reputation wasn't that great to begin with."

"Yes, it is. You're that cool girl who does her own thing. You're different. You stand out. I just blend into the background. No one notices me."

"That's not true, Harry."

"Sure, it is."

Our pizza came and we ate in silence for a few moments before I excused myself to go to the bathroom. I must have the worst timing ever, because on the way there, I spotted Santiago at the To-Go counter handing the cashier a twenty.

I didn't want to act like I didn't see him and keep walking, so I went over reluctantly.

"Hey, Santiago."

He scowled. "I'm just picking up our dinner order," he answered quickly as if he had to explain himself.

Okay, I hadn't asked him that, but whatever.

"We missed you at school today."

He looked straight ahead. Why wouldn't he look at me?

He cleared his throat. "Yeah, I had a sore throat…and a fever…and a stomach ache…and some kind of virus, but I'm fine now."

"Wow, you sure got over all that quickly."

A man placed a pizza box in front of Santiago. "You calling me a liar?"

"That's not what I said at all. Santiago, what's your problem?"

He rolled his eyes as the man handed him his change. "I don't have a problem. What's your problem?"

"I don't have a problem either, but you've been acting weird ever since Harry and I started fake-dating."

Santiago scoffed. "Fake-dating. Right. The two of you looked all too happy to fake-date when Ava brought it up."

Huh? "Santiago, you're imagining things. Anyway, why would that make you mad? Is it because…"

He narrowed his eyes at me. "Because what?"

Suddenly I felt ashamed to say what I had to say. "Because maybe you like me, as in like me-like me."

He smirked. "Where would you get an idea like that? I don't like you-like you."

He was lying and doing a bad job of it.

"Look, Santiago, it's okay. But it's not fair for you to be mad at me for what I'm trying to do to help Harry win the election. And if you like me, you should just say so. I'm not a mind reader."

Santiago shoved his change into his pocket and grabbed the pizza box from the counter. "I don't like you-like you and right about now, I don't even like you as a friend. You and Harry could get married, have a bunch of little red-headed geniuses, and live happily ever after for all I care. Just leave me out of it."

Whoa.

He stormed out of the restaurant and to his mom's car waiting at the curb.

I sighed. If Santiago liked me, why could he tell other people, but not me? We had been friends since the first grade.

I tried to shake him off and made my way to the restroom. When I got back to the table, the pizza was already there, but Harry hadn't started eating without me. Whoever had taught him how to be a gentleman had done a very good job.

"Sorry, I took so long."

Harry smiled. "No problem. Here, let me serve you the first slice." I watched him carefully cut a slice of pizza and slide it onto my plate; then he refilled my glass with Sprite. I had to admit, a girl could get used to that kind of treatment.

Harry and I talked about our families and our plans for high school next year. We had fallen so deep in conversation I had forgotten about all the Nosey Nellies and Looky-Loos sitting around us in awe of the newest couple of Lincoln Middle. Once we were done, Mrs. Kline dropped me off at home because Harry insisted. He even walked me to the door.

He stared down at his shoes. "I had a good time, Bex."

"Me too, Harry."

He laughed to himself. "Forgive me for saying this, but I'm kind of bummed that the election will be over in two days. Then you won't be my girlfriend anymore."

I felt my face burning and I didn't even want to imagine how red I must have been turning in that moment. "Oh," was all I could say. Smooth move, Bex.

"Okay, well, see you tomorrow," Harry said.

"Okay." We stood in awkward silence for a moment and then Harry gave me a quick peck on the cheek before running off the porch.

I touched my cheek and let myself into the house. I leaned against the door thinking about what had just happened.

Someone gasped from the top of the stairs. I glanced up to see my little sister, Priscilla, and Penelope watching me.

"What's wrong with her?" Ray asked.

"She must have eaten some bad pizza," Penelope answered.

"You guys don't know anything," Priscilla said. "That look is the look of love. Bex is in love."

"Ewwwwww!" Ray shrieked.

I ignored them and the fact that they were talking to me as if I wasn't there. Priscilla was wrong though. I wasn't in love in Harry, but I did like him. Dare I say that I might have even liked him-liked him.

12

Rock the Vote
#TeamHarry

Journal Entry #9

Who knew that a fake date could be so much fun? Harry is a great guy and whoever ends up real dating him is going to be a lucky girl. Another boy, on the other hand, is totally stressing me out. I think he likes me, but lately he's been

acting like he hates me. What am I supposed to do with that?

Thursday morning Harry presented me with a bouquet of sunflowers.

"Now that I've gotten to know you a little better, you don't seem like a rose kind of girl. I thought you'd like sunflowers."

He was right. They were one of my favorite colors and absolutely beautiful. Although the gesture was totally sweet of him, by lunch I wanted to chuck the flowers into my locker for two reasons—one, I was tired of carrying them and two, I was tired of everyone staring at me and making googly eyes. Whenever a girl received flowers or balloons from a boy at school, it made her feel special mostly because everyone in the hallways knew that someone liked her. On the other hand, I didn't care much for people staring at me, especially when I knew that the whole thing between Harry and me was a sham.

I almost had a heart attack on my way to the cafeteria when Scary Sherry grasped my arm with her cold, clammy hand. I wished she would stop doing that.

"Everyone I ask has said they were voting for Harry. He's definitely getting more of the girl vote. Everyone thinks he's cute and sweet and they really like his new look. See?"

I looked where Sherry pointed. A small knot formed in my throat as Harry walked down the hallway surrounded by a group of girls. They were laughing and fawning all over him as if he were some kind of celebrity. Seriously?

"Excuse me, Sherry," I said as I marched toward Harry and the group of girls. They had a lot of nerve. Sure, Harry and I were only fake-dating, but they didn't know that.

A few of the girls backed away as I approached. They even looked a little afraid. Sometimes my size did come in handy.

I cleared my throat. "Harry Kline, I've been waiting for you forever. Where have you been?" I lied. I didn't know why, but I was a little angry at Harry although he hadn't done anything wrong.

"I'm sorry, Bex," he said, offering me his arm. "I was just talking to some of my constituents and making sure I had their votes for tomorrow."

Well, I guess that was kind of important.

I took his arm. "Okay, but your favorite constituent is hungry and they're serving pizza sticks today." Ava would have been proud of me for that one.

Harry grinned. "Well, let's go then. Later, ladies."

The girls looked a little sad. A couple of them scowled at me. Were they actually jealous of me? I'd never thought that would happen in my lifetime.

"You know," Harry said as we walked, "we have the debate during sixth period. It would be great if you could sit in the front row so I can see you for support."

"Sure," I could do that. Was this what it was like to be a first lady?

In the cafeteria, Harry and I sat at the table with my friends, but Santiago was suspiciously missing.

"He said he had some work to do in the production room," Jeeves explained, but I knew Santiago was avoiding me. I hate to admit that I didn't spend too much time thinking about Santiago. The more time I spent with Harry, the more I liked him-liked him.

The eighth-graders were all too happy to be missing our sixth-period classes in order to attend the presidential debate in the auditorium. Personally, I couldn't get too excited because I was so nervous for Harry. He was a great speaker, but this was a debate and Kristen Lee could be ruthless. I worried that Harry wouldn't be able to hold his own against her and that would lose him some votes.

I sat in the front row with my friends just as I promised Harry. Cordelia Richards, the captain of the debate team, would read the questions to Harry and Kristen and they would each have a minute to answer.

Three podiums were set up on the stage and Cordelia took the one in the middle while Harry and Kristen took the ones on either side of her. Harry looked at me nervously and I gave him a thumbs-up.

They did a coin flip to see who would answer first. Kristen won the toss-up.

"First question," Cordelia began, "How can we as a student body be sure that you'd represent the general population? Kristen?"

Kristen didn't seem as confident as she usually did. She must have noticed that Harry was getting more and more popular by the minute. She smiled and glanced around the auditorium. "From the beginning I've stated that my goal was to be everybody's president. I want every student, every club, and every activity to be equally represented."

What? When had she ever said that?

"I will make sure that all voices are heard from the academic clubs to sports to the hobby clubs. I will listen to all your needs and concerns and do my best to serve you."

If I were Cordelia I would have moved out of the way. Lightning was going to strike Kristen at any minute.

"Believe me when I say that I love and care about each and every one of you. I'd like the chance to show you that if you would elect me your president."

Anybody with half a brain wouldn't buy that. All I could think about was her threatening to make our lives miserable that day in the locker room. She was a humongous liar! I had the urge to shout that out, but Principal Radcliff had stated before the debate began that there was to be no heckling, so I controlled myself, but it wasn't easy.

Cordelia even rolled her eyes. "Thanks, Kristen. Harry, same question."

"You can be sure that I would represent the general population because I am the general population. I'm not a jock or a popular kid or the kid who stands out. I'm the normal kid who often gets overlooked and I think a lot of kids in this room feel the same way. Since I know what it's like to feel like your voice or opinion doesn't matter, I will do my best to ensure that everyone gets his or her say."

Now *that* was a genuine answer. Harry received a lot of applause after that, more than he had received after his introduction speech.

Kristen looked peeved. I was sure that her real personality was about to show at any moment.

"Thank you, Harry," Cordelia said. "The next question goes to Kristen. 'What three things will you accomplish by May so that we can rate you as either successful or unsuccessful? ' "

Kristen took a deep breath. "Well number one, I've already been coming up with ideas for our winter dance. The theme will be Winter in London. We can even get a Buckingham Palace backdrop. Second, I will make sure that *every* sports team gets cuter uniforms and last, get the library to get issues of our favorite teen magazines so we can read them for free."

I shook my head. Kristen still didn't get it. These kids needed a president who cared about more than dances and cute uniforms.

"Harry's answer was sweet and simple. I will institute a peer tutoring program, more fundraisers so that *all* clubs can get the supplies they need, and more social activities besides dances."

Next, Cordelia asked a question about frog dissection in science class, which apparently is a hot topic among my fellow classmates. Frog Boy got the Look of Death from Principal Radcliff for cheering when both Harry and Kristen said they would try to stop the practice.

Harry trumped Kristen with every answer he gave and I hoped the debate had earned him more points and that the kids could see through Kristen's fakeness.

By the end of the day, I had a full-blown crush. I thought I was the only one who knew about my secret crush until Marishca, Lily-Rose, and Chirpy cornered me in the girl's locker room after PE.

"Bex Carter, you are absolutely glowing," Lily-Rose announced.

I looked down at myself. "What? What does that mean?"

"It means you're in love," Marishca replied, "or falling in it. We see the way you look at Harry."

"And the way he looks at you," Chirpy added. "You guys are *fake*-dating aren't you?"

Who was I kidding? I couldn't hide anything from my best friends, especially not a brand-spanking-new crush.

"Okay, I really, really like him and I think he likes me. He kissed me on my cheek last night and he told me he wished that we were really dating."

The girls squealed. Everyone was staring at us, so I lowered my voice. "Anyway, yes, I like-like Harry Kline."

The girls squealed again except for Chirpy who frowned. "But what about Santiago?"

Everyone fell silent. Santiago was a good friend to all of us and none of us wanted to see him hurt.

I shrugged. "I don't know what to do about Santiago. He hasn't told me that he likes me and last night he said he didn't even want to be friends and of course today he's been totally avoiding me."

Chirpy sighed. "Look, we all love Santiago, but if Bex likes Harry and Harry likes her, they should go out and not feel guilty about it. Santiago will get over it—eventually."

Chirpy was right, but it sounded wrong. I didn't want my friend to be hurt on account of me, but what was I supposed to do? I mean, if he liked me-liked me, he should just come out and say it.

Lily-Rose narrowed her eyes at me. "I think the important question here is, what if Santiago were to ask you out? What would you say?"

I looked down at the ground. I liked Santiago. He was cool, funny, always nice to me, and even a little cute. It was hard for me to think of him that way because we had been friends for so long. If Lily-Rose had asked me that question a few days ago, the answer would have been an absolute, positive yes, but now that Harry was in the picture, things were different. "I-I don't know."

And that was the honest truth.

Friday morning both Kristen and Harry delivered their final speeches on the morning news before the students voted in their first-period classes. I had my fingers crossed that Harry would win. He would make a wonderful president and Kristen Lee was going to turn our eighth-grade class into her very own social club.

I totally tuned Kristen out, but when it was Harry's turn, I was all ears. As he spoke, I couldn't help but notice how handsome he was and how sincere his words were. He was just a good guy who wanted to make the school a better place and whenever I was with him, he treated me like gold. Even though Harry wasn't really my boyfriend, I felt like a very lucky girl in that moment.

When Mrs. Conway passed out the ballot sheets, it only took me a second to check the box next to Harry's name. I closed my eyes and said a silent prayer that maybe just maybe he would win, and maybe for once, I would win and officially be the first lady.

The voting results were being read in sixth period. I wished that Harry and I had that class together so that I could be with him, either to celebrate his win, or to console him if he lost. I sank down in my seat as I waited for Principal Radcliff to tell us whether or not our hard work had paid off.

I sat patiently as he announced the winners of the other offices. "Class recorder, Claire Hutchins." I wondered if I would have won that position if I had actually run for it instead of trying to one-up Ava. "Class treasurer, Max Hayfield. Class Secretary, Mikah Mooney, Vice-President, Sophia Mills."

Principal Radcliff held a white envelope in front of him and took a deep breath. "Drum roll, please." Somewhere in the office someone made a faint-sounding drum roll as Principal Radcliff ripped the envelope open. Ladies and gentlemen, your new eighth-grade president is—"

He paused and it seemed like forever.

"Come on, Principal Radcliff," I whispered to myself.

"Mr. Harry Kline!"

The room erupted in cheers. I smiled, relieved that we wouldn't have to endure Kristen Lee's reign of terror for the rest of our middle school lives. I was happy for Harry and wished I could see him right then.

After school I had to wade through the thick crowd of students trying to congratulate Harry on his win. A couple of weeks ago you would have never imagined that a shy, quiet kid like Harry Kline would be getting mobbed by everyone trying to talk to him all at once.

Kristen Lee barreled her way through the crowd making a stink-face. "I hate this school! This will be the worst, most boring year ever! Just wait!"

Sheesh. Talk about a sore loser.

Finally, I made my way to Harry and to my surprise, he grabbed me and hugged me tightly. Okay, so I know when people are really, really happy they do things they wouldn't normally do. I would have hugged him back or said something, but I couldn't breathe.

Harry let me go and looked at me. "Thanks so much, Bex. I couldn't have done it without you and your friends."

Just then Ava G. broke in between us. "I knew it. Didn't I tell you to leave everything to me and I would lead you to victory? I never lose anything."

Yeah, except for her mind occasionally. The way she was talking, you would have thought that she had done everything on her own.

"Anyway," she continued, "you know that I will find any reason to throw a fabulous party. I want to throw you a victory party at my club house tomorrow evening."

"That sounds awesome," Harry said. Then he turned to me. "Bex, will you be my date?"

Ava jumped in before I could even answer because she is in a permanent state of super-rudeness. "Uh, Harry, the election's over. You won. You don't have to pretend that you like Bex anymore."

"Who's pretending?"

If I were the type of girl who swooned, I would have done it right there. Ava frowned, looking confused as if it were impossible for a guy to like me for real.

"Sure, whatever. Anyway, the party starts at six." Then she wandered off still looking perplexed.

Harry turned to me. "My mother is throwing me a small party tonight at my house, just the family. She's making some Italian food. Want to come? I would like for her to meet you."

Meeting his family? This was a bit sudden.

"Um, sure. How did your mom know you were going to win?"

Harry grinned. "She didn't. She was planning the party either way."

"What time?"

"Seven."

"Okay, see you then." I turned to leave, but Harry stopped me.

"Bex, you know Ava's right. You don't have to pretend to like me anymore if you really don't."

I looked down at the ground and blushed. "Who's pretending?"

I had to set things right with Santiago before going home that day. I couldn't go another day with him ignoring me and being in a miserable mood. I knew I'd find him in the computer lab working on something.

He was the only one in the room since it was Friday afternoon and everyone else had fled the school as if it were on fire. He didn't look up or say a word as I came in. I sat at the computer next to his. "What are you doing? It's time to go home."

"I wanted to update the school website with our new student government positions," he mumbled. "Congratulations, by the way."

"We all had a hand in helping Harry win," I reminded him.

"But now Harry's super-popular and you're dating him which makes you super-popular."

"We're not dating."

"But you want to date. I can tell."

I didn't want to talk about Harry. I wanted to talk about me and Santiago. "Santiago, what do I have to do for you to not be angry with me?"

"Nothing, Bex. I shouldn't have been angry with you in the first place. I guess I was angry at myself for not making a move sooner. I should have known that sooner or later somebody else would."

So did he like me-like me or what? "Does that mean—"

"I think you know what it means, but it doesn't matter now. Harry's a nice guy. I'm sure you two will be very happy."

"But—"

Santiago took his headphones from around his neck and placed them over his ears. "I have to get back to work."

I had gotten my answer. I knew why Santiago had been angry and how he felt about me, but still, things weren't right between us and I didn't like it.

13

The President's Ball

—feeling in ♡

Journal Entry #10

I'm super nervous right now. Even
though Harry and I aren't officially
boyfriend and girlfriend, I want to make a
good impression on his family. After all, if
Harry and I get married one day, they'll be
my in-laws. Okay, okay, I know I'm getting
way ahead of myself but it could happen.

Friday night Aunt Jeanie dropped me off at the Kline's. I
was greeted at the door by Harry's father who was an older

version of Harry. Harry came downstairs and introduced me to his younger brother and sister, his grandmother, and his aunt and uncle. Everyone was welcoming and friendly. Just as I was about to take a seat on the couch, Mrs. Kline stuck her head out of the kitchen.

"Oh, good, Bex, you're here. Come in the kitchen and give me a hand."

The only thing I knew how to cook was grilled cheese so I wasn't sure how much help she expected me to give her.

She went to stirring a pot on the stove. "Hon, grab a spatula from the dish drainer and cut the lasagna into small squares please."

"Sure." That I could handle. I grabbed a spatula and did what she asked me to.

"I'm glad to get to finally meet you. Harry talks about you all the time," Mrs. Kline said. I stole a look at her as I worked. She wore a red apron with white trim and had dark curly hair gathered into a ponytail at the top of her head.

"Oh, he does?"

"Yes, he has for years."

Years? Harry and I had only been going out for a few days.

She waltzed past me to grab something from the fridge. "I know all about how good you are at soccer and a food fight you started—"

"Wait, that wasn't really my fault."

"It's okay, dear. I was young once. Anyway, I know about how you stand up to bullies and how you led the girls in your school through a boycott. Every time he tells me a story, I say, 'Bex sounds like my kind of girl. I have to meet her. ' "

I blushed. It wasn't every day that someone called me "their kind of girl."

I couldn't believe that Harry had been telling his mother about me all this time. I was flattered, but it felt kind of weird at the same time.

"I'm really glad Harry won the election," I said, trying to change the subject. "He's going to make a wonderful president."

"He will. I'm so happy for him."

We chatted a little more and I helped Mrs. Kline bring the food to the dinner table. We sat around and ate and for a few moments, I really felt like part of the Kline family.

After dinner Harry and I sat on his front porch while we waited for Aunt Jeanie to come pick me up.

"Your family's cool," I told him.

"Thanks. Hopefully I get to meet yours soon."

I shrugged. "If you want, but I'm telling you, they're nothing like your family. They're nuts."

Harry laughed. "Well, if they're anything like you, they're great."

That was when it happened. Harry leaned in and kissed me straight on the lips! I didn't even see it coming. Harry was some kind of kiss-stealing ninja.

I didn't know what to do so I looked straight ahead. From the corner of my eye I could see that Harry was doing the same.

"I hope that was okay," he said.

"Yeah," was all I could manage as Aunt Jeanie pulled into the driveway. "See you tomorrow night."

"Okay. See you."

As I climbed into the front seat, I couldn't wait to get home and call my friends. They would flip.

"Have fun?" Aunt Jeanie asked as she backed out of the driveway.

"Yes. I had a nice time."

"Harry seems like a nice boy."

"He is," I replied. "He's a very nice boy." Harry was more than a nice boy, but the butterflies in my stomach were fluttering their wings so rapidly that I couldn't think of the right words.

The Tribe came over on Saturday afternoon so that we could get ready for Harry's victory party together. Ava had tried to say that they weren't invited, but Harry insisted that everyone who worked on his campaign team be there and that they could bring dates. That made me like him even more.

I didn't care much for dresses, but I figured I could deal with it for one night. I knew that Harry would be dressed up so I wanted to look nice since I would be his date. Lily-Rose was going with Maverick, Marishca was going with Caleb, and Chirpy finally worked up the nerve to ask out Mikey. I was so proud of her and now we would all be paired up.

Chirpy flat-ironed half of my head and then passed the iron to Lily-Rose when she got tired. Tackling my hair was no small feat. While they worked on my hair, Marishca applied my makeup.

"You look beautiful, Bex, like a real princess."

Once they were done and I checked myself out in the mirror, I had to agree. I wore a pale pink dress that came out at the knees. Since it was spaghetti-strapped, Aunt

Jeanie insisted that I wear a tiny matching jacket over it. I didn't have a problem with that. Once we were pleased with our appearance, Sophia drove us to Ava's clubhouse since Aunt Jeanie and Uncle Bob had already left to spend the evening with some friends.

As usual, Ava had gone all out. She had the party decked out in red, white, and blue and a huge banner that read "Congratulations, Harry!"

When I arrived I had one dance with Harry; then he was whisked off to take pictures. You would have thought that he had just become the president of the United States the way some people were acting.

Since my friends had dates, I spent a great deal of time by myself. I wished Santiago had come, but I hadn't expected him to show up. He always seemed to be there when I was feeling bummed and at that moment I was feeling a little left out.

A girl was interviewing Harry for her blog and then for some reason, Mrs. Groves insisted that Harry do an acceptance speech. After the speech, he disappeared so I made myself a plate of chicken fingers and sat in a corner.

A few minutes later Chirpy joined me. "Why are you sitting all by yourself, Bex?"

"My date is busy," I said.

Chirpy looked sad for me. "Oh. That stinks. Come hang out with me and Mikey."

I had no interest in being a third wheel. "That's okay, Chirp. Really, I'm good. Go have fun. Don't worry about me."

She left but came back a minute later with Marishca and Lily-Rose because I have the best friends ever. Lily-Rose put her hands on her hips. "The Bex Carter I know wouldn't be sitting around at a party moping because her date is busy. She'd be on the dance floor turning it up. Let's dance!"

They pulled me onto the dance floor and we danced like fools until we were tired. I had almost forgotten about Harry not being around—almost. Aunt Jeanie called to tell me that she and Uncle Bob were waiting outside so I had to go. I looked around for Harry to tell him good-bye, but he was still nowhere to be found. I sent him a text that I was leaving. A little later he texted, *"So, sorry we didn't get much time together. Things got busy. Some date I am, right? Call you later."*

His text was so sweet I couldn't even be mad at him. After all, the party was about him and his victory.

14

Boys!!!

—feeling angry ☹

Grrrrrrr!!!!!!!

Journal Entry #11
As far as love goes, I give up. That is all.

Whose great idea was it to create boys? I guess we kind of need them or people would become extinct, but why do they have to cause so much trouble? I don't get them at all. One day they act one way and then the next they're like totally different people. Somebody please explain boys to me!

Okay, I'll calm down and back up a bit. After Harry hadn't called like he said he would, I was a little worried.

Then Sunday afternoon Aunt Jeanie told me that a very well-dressed young man was standing on the front porch. I was a little happy, but I was also a little confused.

"Hey, Harry," I said as I stepped onto the porch. "What's up?"

He handed me a single sunflower that he had been holding behind his back. I took the flower, but something was wrong. Harry didn't seem like his normal self.

He pointed to the porch swing. "Bex, let's sit down."

If I ever teach you anything, let it be this—if someone ever tells you to sit down before they tell you something, whatever they have to tell you is going to be bad. Really bad.

I took a seat and held my breath. What could he possibly have to tell me that could be that bad? Was his family moving away? Did he have a terminal disease? What? He was looking as if somebody had died.

"What is it, Harry?"

He looked out into the front yard. "Bex, you and I had some fun times together, but we were never officially boyfriend and girlfriend, right?"

"I guess not." I certainly thought we were heading in that direction, but I didn't say it out loud.

"Good because you should know that last night Ava T. and I started going out."

"What?" I didn't mean to sound as surprised and angry as I did, but that had totally taken me by surprise. "You and Ava T.?"

"Yeah, she's really popular and since I'm the president now it just makes sense that I should be with someone like that. Ava G. explained it to me. She knew what I needed to do to win the election so I trust her advice."

Ava G. I could just feel my hands squeezing her little neck. Would this girl ever stop ruining my life?

Harry looked extremely guilty. "Y-you don't mind do you, Bex? If it's going to make you angry, I'll call the whole thing off."

"Do I mind? Of course not. You two could get married and have a bunch of little mean girl-geniuses for all I care!"

Harry frowned. "Really? Because you sound kind of mad."

"Now, why on earth would I be mad?" Wow. Even smart boys could be completely clueless.

"I'm sorry, Bex. I know this is a really jerky thing to do and you're an awesome girl. I don't want to hurt your feelings and I really do like you—"

"But..."

"But I think things happen for a reason. I know of a really cool kid who likes you, so maybe this wasn't meant to be."

"Harry, I want you to leave."

"I'm really sorry, Bex. Can we still be friends?"

"Just go." I didn't see myself being friends with Harry any time soon. I felt lied to and betrayed. All week he had totally acted as if he really liked me and then all of a sudden he was dating someone else. He'd made me feel like a fool and I never wanted to see him again.

"Okay, Bex. I'm really sorry. I didn't mean to hurt you. See you around, I guess."

I said nothing as I watched him walk down the sidewalk. I don't know how he had gotten to Aunt Jeanie's or how he was going home, but at that moment I didn't care.

I ran up to my room and buried my face in my pillow before the tears flowed. Was this how I had made Santiago feel—angry and rejected? Even though I hadn't meant to or really done anything to cause it, I felt guilty. I had to make things right with my friend sooner rather than later.

Mrs. Ortiz told me that Santiago had gone to the park down the street from his house to shoot some hoops so I rode my bike there. I found Santiago playing by himself. When he took a shot I caught the rebound.

"I'll play you," I said.

He waved his hand. "I'm tired. I'm going home."

He turned to walk away, but I had to stop him this time. "Santiago, I'm sorry. I'm not even sure of what I did but I'm sorry."

"You didn't do anything, Bex. I like you, okay, a lot. And it's hard for me to see you be someone else's girlfriend. It's hard for me to even be around you right now."

"I'm not someone else's girlfriend. Harry and I are not going out and we never will." Just the mention of that boy's name made my blood boil. I wanted to pretend that the basketball was his head.

"Oh," Santiago said. "That's too bad."

"It just wasn't meant to be," I said. "Anyway, are we good? If we weren't friends anymore I don't know if I could take it."

"Yeah, we're good," he replied. "Sorry for how I've been acting. It wasn't your fault."

"It's okay. I just hope you feel the same way after I whoop your butt one-on-one."

Santiago snatched the ball from me and smirked. "Oh yeah, let's go."

We played a quick game of one-on-one and I won, although I kind of think he let me win. Either way, it was good to have my friend back.

"I know!" Lily-Rose shouted on the other end of the phone. "We should cover his entire body with honey and lay him down on a giant ant pile and then we can pluck his toenails off with pliers!"

Marishca, Chirpy, and I were silent on our ends of the phone.

"Come back, Lily-Rose," I said gently. I appreciated her having my back, but sheesh.

"I can't believe that creep," Chirpy said. "I thought he was a nice guy."

"Yeah," Marishca added. "He shouldn't have led you on only to go out wiz someone else."

I sighed. "He did offer to call the whole thing off with Ava T."

Lily-Rose snorted. "Yeah, that's what every girl wants. A guy to date her so she won't be mad at him."

"It's okay. I'm over it," I lied. The truth was that I thought my heart was really broken. I tried not to be hurt or angry, but I couldn't help it. I hadn't told Aunt Jeanie all the details, but she knew that something was wrong with me and she promised me that with time whatever it was would pass. She was a lot older and wiser than me, so I believed her.

"I wouldn't be too mad about it," Marishca said. "Ava T. is going to eventually rip his heart out and stomp on it. Those Avas are ruthless."

I agreed. As horrible as it was, I hoped that Ava T. would break his heart and make him feel the way he'd made me feel and then maybe he'd never do that to another girl again.

As we talked more about the victory party, I heard the doorbell ring. A few seconds later Sophia knocked on my bedroom door to tell me that I had a visitor.

"I have to go, guys. See you tomorrow."

After I hung up with my friends and ran downstairs, I discovered Santiago standing on my porch. When I had left him at the park he told me that he had to go home to get some work done for his business. I wondered what he was doing at my house.

"Hey, Santiago. Is everything okay?"

He nodded.

"Want to come in?"

He shook his head. "I'd rather not. This is kind of a private conversation."

I shut the door behind me a little afraid of what he had to say. "What's up?"

He cleared his throat a whole bunch of times before he spoke. "Um, I'm kind of scared to say this…"

"We've been friends forever. You can tell me anything."

"Yeah, we're friends—that's the problem. We're friends and for a while I've been thinking that I'd like to be more than friends."

My heart started to race. "Oh." I know, I know. I really need to work on my responses.

"It's okay if you don't feel the same way. I just wanted to get that off my chest. I like you a lot, Bex. I think you're the most awesome girl I know."

"Oh." I wished I could say something else, but aside from that, I was kind of speechless.

Thankfully, Santiago kept talking. "Sooooo, I was thinking that on Friday we could go to Bumpers."

Bumpers was a place that had go-carts and a bowling alley. A lot of kids from our school hung out there on the weekend.

"That sounds like fun," I said. "Is that a date?"

Santiago looked down at his sneakers. "Yeah, it's a date; that is unless you don't want it to be."

"No, it can be a date," I answered.

Santiago smiled, looking relieved. "Good. I guess I'll see you in school tomorrow."

"Yeah."

I watched him walk away. I liked Santiago. Liked-liked him and I hoped being more than friends wouldn't destroy our friendship.

Harry Kline was right about one thing—what's meant to be will be. Ava T. dumped him after exactly three weeks because he'd broken out with a bad case of acne. Ava G. had decided that no Ava could date a boy with blemishes, whether he was class president or not, so Harry was history. Knowing about their breakup didn't make me feel as good as I thought it would. As far as Santiago and I go—things are great. We're having a lot of fun together, so we'll see.

I'll definitely keep you posted. A lot has happened in the past month so I have a few lessons for you this time.

Life Lessons from Bex:

1. What's meant to be will be whether you want it to be or not.

2. Don't even try to understand boys. (Put a star next to this one.)

3. If you run for something important, make sure it's for the right reasons.

Look out for Bex Carter #6: So Scandalous coming soon!!!

Other books in the Bex Carter Series:

Made in the USA
San Bernardino, CA
13 January 2017